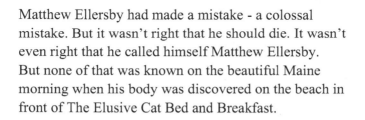

Dark and Stormy Night Mystery

Poisoned Petit Fours

By Sara Bourgeois

Chapter 1

Matthew Ellersby had made a mistake - a colossal mistake. But it wasn't right that he should die. It wasn't even right that he called himself Matthew Ellersby. But none of that was known on the beautiful Maine morning when his body was discovered on the beach in front of The Elusive Cat Bed and Breakfast.

When Jan Cathcart is forced out of her life by a series of unfortunate events, she lands at her sister's popular bed and breakfast. Little does she know that her move will place her right in the middle of a murder mystery.

The local police made the wrong call about the crime, but Jan knows in her heart that the man was murdered. Can she solve the crime before the small-town rumor mill destroys her sister's beloved business?

* * *

Jan Cathcart stared at the ceiling in her room. It was a plain white ceiling showing some signs of age in the discoloring by the closet door. The center light and fan were both off. The morning sun was coming up and lightened the room enough for her to see the start of a cobweb near the center of the fan. She should check the other rooms. She should do some cleaning. She should get out of bed.

August 8 - three months to the day. Three months since that conversation and she could still remember every word. Three months since her life went to pieces. And maybe she had caused it. Maybe she was wrong.

She threw her legs off the edge of the bed and angrily yanked off her pajama top. Stop doing that! It was over. Done with. Get dressed and get to work. She quickly grabbed her jeans from the floor where she had dropped them the previous evening. She rummaged in her drawer for a clean t-shirt. In the bathroom, she brushed her short dark hair with abrupt strokes and pushed it behind her ears. It would do.

There was no sound from the other bedroom as she slipped on her sandals. Not surprising. Lolinda James was never an early riser. As she closed the door to the guest house and started along the short pathway to the main house, she saw a tiny gray kitten scurry from the beach to behind the house. She used her key to enter the main house and made her way to the kitchen. Her sister was already working on the breakfasts for the guests. "What can I do?"

Lois looked up from the pan that she was stirring on the stove. "Good morning. I didn't get all the tables set if you could do that."

Jan took the necessary silverware and plates from the cupboards and went out into the large dining area. It was separated from the kitchen by a half-wall topped by the counter. That's where Lois would put the food when ready so that each guest could help themself. Jan went around laying out the places. There were two round tables in the center of the room, which comfortably seated four people, and two tables for couples by the front windows, overlooking the beach. It was a pleasant room and was now filling with the lovely smells from the kitchen. Jan did her job mechanically. Focus on the proper placement of the forks and spoons. Make sure the sugar and creamer bowls were full. Square off the napkins. Don't think about the date or the conversation.

"Jan," Lois called from the kitchen. "Could you come stir this for a moment while I chop some more mushrooms? Doesn't look like I have enough."

Jan put the remaining dishes on the counter and went into the kitchen. She took over the spoon in the lightly bubbling pot on the stove. It was a rich creamy sauce with lots of mushrooms, to her eye. But her sister was the cook. And good thing, too. Jan could handle simple meals for herself, but she thought of cooking, and eating, as a waste of time and energy. She never understood the pleasure that first her mother and now Lois got from hours of preparation for something that would be eaten and gone in about thirty minutes.

Lois added the extra mushrooms and took over the stirring again. "Thanks. I really need to do a good clean of this kitchen. Those petit fours sure made a mess."

Jan looked around the spotless kitchen. True, there were still some pans in the sink and some canisters on the counter from the baking the day before. But it was hardly a mess. Still, she had enjoyed those little pastries and wanted to be helpful. "I'll give you a hand after breakfast. Also, I noticed a cobweb forming on my ceiling fan and thought I should check all the fixtures and fans around the house."

"That's a good idea. Nobody new in or out today. Just the same crowd for the rest of the week."

"I told the Tiptons that I would show them the spot up the beach where they can rent kayaks for the day. Looks like another beautiful calm day. By the way, I saw Kitty Jr. running up from the beach this morning."

Lois smiled and moved the pot off the stove, replacing it with a large frying pan. Jan went back to setting the tables. The little kitten's name wasn't really Kitty Jr. In fact, it had no name. Nor did its mother. The cat had come with the place when Lois and their mother had bought it four years ago. Their mother had passed two years back from breast cancer - the one and only time Jan had been to the B&B. The cat was dark gray with white splotches, but the kitten was gray all over. The kitten had appeared around the same time that Jan had shown up at the door, unannounced. Both the cats were feral and came and went as they pleased. Lois left a bowl of kibbles and water out back, but no one had ever managed to pet either one of them. Although the two Tipton kids had tried. The cats stayed elusive and thus the name - The Elusive Cat Bed and Breakfast.

Jan looked up as she heard footsteps coming down the stairs. It was the Tiptons, a family of four from California. The mom and kids had driven across the country and arrived more than two weeks ago. The father had come in by taxi from the airport on the weekend. They were a pleasant-looking couple, both tall and blond. The older daughter was also blond, around fifteen and would be turning heads on the beach any day now. Her younger brother was a bit darker and was out for adventure. He was the one pushing for the sea kayak experience.

They all said good morning and headed to the breakfast bar. Lois was setting out the last of the dishes. Today's offerings were blueberry pancakes and a cheese omelet with the creamy mushroom sauce. The boy, Brad, loaded four pancakes on his plate and took one of the maple syrup glass pour bottles to their table. His sister, Josie, took some eggs. The parents took some of each. They had just settled in their seats and started to eat when the Traegers came down. They were a retired couple from Germany, spending one week in Maine before going to New York City. They took their choices from the food and sat at the other round table. As usual, they had their maps and guidebooks with them. Each morning they stayed at the table until they had planned their itinerary for the day. Often, they asked for suggestions from Lois and the other guests. After learning that Jan had only been here for two months, they didn't ask her much, although they were very pleasant. Frau Traeger loved the small shops in the nearby little town of Henry's Harbor. Herr Traeger wanted either the bigger museums in Bar Harbor or to go trekking through Acadia National Park. Usually their itinerary was a compromise. Maybe that's how it happened after thirty or so years of marriage.

Unlikely that Jan and Greg would have ever been able to compromise. No, she wouldn't think about him. He was gone, obliterated from her memories. She wished. She left the breakfast room and returned quickly to the kitchen, starting to vigorously wash the pots and pans left from making breakfast. Lois just left her alone and went to join the guests. They were all down except Mr. Ellersby, who usually went for an early long walk on the

6

beach and ate after everyone else had left. And, of course, Lolinda, who would show up sometime before noon and make no complaints about a quickly microwave reheated breakfast. She had been coming to the B&B for all four years that it had been open. She had her routine and Lois just accommodated her.

Lois was good at adapting herself to others. She had asked Jan in for coffee that morning over two months ago. In the beginning Lois had asked lots of questions. After all, it was a bit strange for her younger sister to show up at her doorstep, suitcase in hand, after they hadn't spoken in two years, since the funeral of their mother. But she had learned not to ask questions because Jan's constant reply was to leave the room and sit on the beach. In the rain, during windstorms, even late at night, she would be there on the beach. So, Lois stopped asking questions. Not even a "How are you?" question in the morning. But Jan knew that she was still asking the questions with her eyes. She wasn't ready yet with any answers. She didn't have any answers herself. She scrubbed harder.

She was interrupted by Brad calling her name. The twelve-year-old was leaning over the breakfast counter. "Jan, when can you take us to the kayak place?"

His mother called, "Brad, she's busy. Leave her alone. I'm sorry, Jan."

"No problem," Jan smiled at Brad. She liked his energy. He reminded her of her students. "They won't open until 9:00. We can go then if you are ready."

"Great! Thanks." He popped back to his table and announced that he was going to the beach. He raced up the stairs to get his swimsuit and towel. As he came back down a moment later, his mother called after him, "Don't go in the water yet. You just ate breakfast and there's no one down there."

"I know, Mom," came floating back through the door as it closed.

His mother shook her head and settled down to finish her breakfast in peace. Her daughter was typing rapidly on her phone and her husband was reading a fishing brochure. But her vision of a peaceful breakfast was soon shattered by the sudden opening of the door. Brad was there, his towel still in his hand, but his face was white, and he was visibly shaking. "Dad!" he yelled. "There's a dead man down on the beach!"

Everyone was on their feet in an instant. Lois was the first out the door because she had been closest. Jan put down her scrub brush and dried her hands, before following the others. Somehow a dead man seemed unexceptional to her today. When she got to the beach, they were all standing around in a circle. Mr. Tipton had rolled the body over and they could see that it was Mr. Ellersby. He was dressed in his usual manner of casual slacks and a designer t-shirt. His clothes were crumpled and covered in sand. His eyes and mouth were open.

Lois saw her coming and said, "Jan, go back to the house and call the sheriff's office. The number is on the fridge."

Sheriff Raymond Nolan arrived with two constables within twenty minutes. No one had moved from their circle on the beach. They reluctantly parted to let the officers in to check the body. The first to stir was Mrs. Tipton, who had her arm around her daughter. "We should go back to the house."

The sheriff looked up from his examination. "That's a good idea. Lois, please escort everyone back to the house. We will be up there soon as we take care of this poor man." He started giving instructions to his constables as they slowly trekked back to the eating room. Lois went into the kitchen to make some fresh coffee. Mrs. Tipton took her two youngsters into the large family room at the back of the house. Brad didn't seem to want to go but his mother took him by the shoulders and led him out. Jan settled herself back in the kitchen, out of the way.

Then she thought of something. She went to Lois. "Shouldn't I tell Lolinda? You know that sometimes she likes to take a morning dip before breakfast."

"Good idea. Yes, tell her and have her come here. I'm sure Ray will want to speak with everyone."

As Jan went out the front door, she saw that one of the constables was still standing over the body while the other was searching the beach. She wondered what they hoped to find. She went back along the pathway to the recessed guest house. Again, she spotted the gray kitten, this time sitting along the path. It melted back into the small bushes as she approached but she could swear it had been watching her and the beach, turning its tiny little head back and forth between the two. She opened the guest house door and knocked on Lolinda's room. It took a couple of firm knocks before she heard movement. Lolinda came to the door in a light pajama set of shorts and top. She was still rubbing her eyes.

"Sorry to disturb you but we've had something rather drastic happen and I wanted to warn you. There's a dead man on the beach, one of the guests, Mr. Ellersby. The police want to talk with us all in the main house."

Lolinda was tall and fit. At fifty-three years of age, it was obvious that she took care of herself. There were no traces yet of gray in her tightly curled black hair and Jan knew, from their shared bathroom, that her hair color was natural. As an actress of long standing, she held herself proudly. But now her expression was one of confusion. "A dead man - Ellersby? Is this a dream? Why would there be a dead man on our beach?"

"No dream, I'm afraid, Ms. Lolinda. This is reality. I'll wait in my room while you get ready."

Jan sat on her bed and looked at the spiderweb. Somehow a dead man seemed to fit in perfectly with the three-month anniversary of the conversation. It had been the death of her life. A corpse was a fitting tribute. And yet, this was reality, as she had told Lolinda. There really was a dead man there. A man who had kept himself private during his few days at the B&B, but he had seemed a nice man, all the same. She had seen him talking briefly with Herr Traeger. She had only exchanged pleasantries with him, but he had been polite, with a sincere though somehow troubled smile. Who was she to judge? She had a troubled smile most of the time herself. But she wasn't dead, not really. And he was. But that could be left to the police. Probably suicide.

Lolinda came to her door, dressed in a flattering pantsuit. They walked silently back to the main house and Jan left her with the others for them to fill her in. She retreated again to the kitchen. Lois was sitting at the small eating table there where they had their meals. She was ceaselessly wiping her hands on a hand towel. "How'd she take it?"

"Hasn't sunk in yet," Jan replied.

"Probably the same for most of us. Poor man. I think I'll bake some bread. People need carbs at a time like this. I suppose we could be here for a while." She got up and started pulling ingredients from the cupboards. Jan went into the breakfast room and started to clear the dishes. Most people had already finished their breakfast. She left the food on the counter in case anyone was hungry. Maybe the constables would want something.

Back in the kitchen, she scraped and rinsed the dishes before loading the dishwasher. Lois was intently measuring flour into several large bowls. "How many loaves are you making?" Jan asked.

"I'll do a cherry loaf, a cinnamon raisin one, a whole wheat one and a honey white."

"That will feed an army," Jan exclaimed.

"We'll freeze what they don't eat. Now, don't mess up my counting. That's four cups for that one, I think." She picked up the bowl and compared it to the one already full. Then she started measuring flour into the next one. Jan left her to her labors.

After finishing with the dishes, she took a cloth to wipe down the tables. More coffee cups were stacked by the machine. Then she went into the family room to see if the family needed anything. She wondered how Brad would be handling his gruesome discovery. Probably better than his mother.

She found the boy sitting in the corner of a couch, with his back half turned towards his mother, who sat near him. His sister was in a large chair by the window, typing on her phone. Mrs. Tipton looked up as she entered and Jan signaled her over with a nod of the head. When the mother approached, Jan said quietly, "I don't want to interfere, Mrs. Tipton. I just wanted you to know that I'm a middle school teacher by profession. I would be happy to speak with Brad if you would like."

She nodded. "Thank you. Maybe he'll talk to you. He just says he's fine but I'm worried."

"No problem. How's Josie handling this?"

"Texting her friends, I think."

"You might want to tell her to keep the details to a minimum. Out of respect for Mr. Ellersby and his family, if he has any."

"Of course. I didn't think of that." She moved off quickly to speak quietly to her daughter.

Jan went over and sat on the other end of the couch from Brad, giving him his space. "You are just fine, aren't you?"

He looked over at her. "That's what I keep saying but she won't believe me."

"Give her a break. She's a mom and they worry. That's what they do."

"Are you a mom?"

"What? All that worry? You got to be kidding. Not me," Jan replied with a grin.

He laughed. Then he stopped abruptly. "Suppose I shouldn't be laughing. Not with him dead and all."

"It's never wrong to laugh," Jan said. "Hope you don't mind my curiosity, but how did you know that he was dead? I mean, he could have been sleeping."

"He was so white and stiff."

"Did you touch him?"

"No. I could just tell. And his eyes. They were creepy."

"What do you mean?"

Brad stared out the window. "They were all filmy and there was sand in them." He rubbed his own eyes. "I knew he was dead. No one could just lie there with sand in their eyes." He rubbed harder.

"Yeah, that would be creepy," Jan kept her voice calm. "But he wouldn't feel it so I guess it doesn't matter. Wouldn't bother him like it does us. I find it helps to remember that. He would never have felt the sand."

Brad's voice was tentative. "I guess that's true. I wonder how he died."

"The police will find out. That's their job. Glad it's not my job. I'd rather wash dishes all day than deal with dead people."

Brad looked at her. "You wash dishes all day?"

"Not usually. Actually, I'm the enemy," she smiled.

"What?"

"I'm a school teacher."

He smiled. "Really? Where do you teach?"

"In California," she replied.

"Hey! That's where I'm from! We live in the Bay Area. Place called Portola Valley."

"I live and teach not far from there. In Palo Alto but you wouldn't be at my school."

"Why not?"

Jan grinned at him. "Because it's an all-girls school."

"All girls? Yuck! All that drama!"

She laughed. "You are so right."

"So are you on vacation, too?"

"Sort of. As you know, Lois is my sister. I'm just here to help out. And to get a break from the kids, not including you and your sister."

"You wash dishes during your vacation? That's a bummer."

"Not that bad. By the way, I guess we'll have to postpone the kayaking to another day. The police will probably want to ask us lots of questions. At least that's what they do on TV."

Brad nodded. "I saw this show and they said that they usually get the most important facts during the first twenty-four hours after a murder. Could he have been murdered?"

"It's a possibility but not likely. Most people die because of accidents. Maybe he went out for a late night swim and went too far out. It's so important for people to know their limitations. But sometimes, as we get older, we think we can do everything that we did when we were kids. I bet you're a really good swimmer."

"Went to the buoy and back twice without a break yesterday."

"Good for you! That's quite the swim. I always grab on to the buoy and take a breather before I head back. And I've never done it twice in a row."

They all looked up as Lois came into the room. "Sheriff Ray would like us all in the breakfast room."

17

They walked out but Brad stayed near Jan. Mrs. Tipton watched from where she sat with her husband and daughter. But she seemed content to let him be.

Sheriff Nolan introduced himself and his constable, Dan Phelps, and thanked them all for waiting for him. "I understand that the deceased has been staying here for a few days. My constable and I would like to ask you a few questions and then we will let you get on with your day. We also ask that you give us a phone number where you can be reached for the next while."

"How did he die?" Mr. Tipton asked.

"We're still getting information, sir. I can't really give you any answers right now. If you please, I would like to speak with Ms. Lois first if there is a private room."

Lois stood up. "We can use the family room in the back." She turned to her guests. "Folks, there's fresh coffee and tea. Just ask Jan if you want any food. I have several different loaves of bread coming soon. I'm sure the sheriff and his men will do everything they can so that you don't lose the whole day. Jan, perhaps you could show Constable Phelps which room Mr. Ellersby was staying in."

"Thank you, Ms. Lois," Sheriff Nolan said. "That would be helpful." He gestured towards the back room and left with Lois.

Jan led the way up the stairs, seeing the guests refilling coffee cups. Lolinda was filling a plate with breakfast. Brad went and grabbed a muffin, then sat beside his dad. After showing the constable the room, she went back down and headed into the kitchen. She kept a close eye on Brad, knowing that he was still processing what he had seen. She saw his father lean over and ask him something. He responded by glaring at his dad and pushing back his chair. She quickly went to the breakfast bar and called, "Brad, could you give me a hand?"

He turned his back on his father and came quickly into the kitchen. Jan could see that he was angry but she just said, "I gather from our earlier conversation that you're not a huge fan of washing dishes. How about unloading dishwashers? Can you handle that?"

"Sure. Just tell me where to stack them."

She showed him where to put the dishes and silverware and he started working. She kept working on the pans from yesterday's baking. She had left them soaking in order to make them easier to clean. Now she refilled the sink with hot water. Then she noticed that Brad had stopped with a glass in his hand. He was staring out at his family's table, where his mother was leaning over his sister.

Jan moved beside him and said, "What's the matter, Brad?"

"Could we ask Josie to help?"

"You mean your mom is worrying again."

He gave her a slight smile. "Yeah."

Jan went back to the counter. "Josie, if you're available, we could use your help, too."

The girl came as quickly as her brother. "What do you need, Jan?"

"How are you at organizing things?"

"Okay, I guess."

"See all those canisters and measuring things. I have no clue where they go. My sister wisely keeps me out of the kitchen except for washing pots. Do you think you could snoop through all those cupboards and figure out where they go?"

"Sure." She started to open cupboard doors. "Why aren't you allowed in the kitchen? Don't you do some of the cooking?"

"You kids really don't want to taste my cooking," Jan told them seriously. "This place would empty so fast if Lois let me cook. We'll leave the cooking to her."

"So what's your job?" Josie asked.

"She's a school teacher," Brad replied.

"Really? So why are you here?"

"On vacation, like you," Jan replied.

"But I always see you washing the dishes and cleaning the tables," Josie objected. "That's not a vacation."

Jan smiled. "Don't see why not. After all, you guys are unloading the dishwasher and straightening the kitchen. Vacations come in all shapes and sizes."

The kids grinned and got back to work. Lois came in soon and praised them for their industriousness. She said that Sheriff Nolan wanted to speak with Brad. "Your mom or dad can go in with you."

21

He thought for a moment. "I'd rather have Jan come with me, if that's okay?" he asked, looking at Jan.

"That will be up to your mom. I'll go ask her." Jan went into the breakfast room and asked Mrs. Tipton to come over to the window to speak with her. The woman looked drawn with worry. "Mrs. Tipton," Jan began.

"Please, call me Judy," the woman said. "How's Brad?"

"He's still processing what happened. He's coping as well as he can."

"Thanks for asking him to help. He was so jumpy."

"He saw something that he found very disturbing. But he also needs to know that he is in control - of the situation and of himself. He is a child but he sees himself as a man. I'm just trying to get him to talk about it in little ways so that he can put what he saw in perspective. He's a strong kid and he's doing really well." She took a deep breath. "The police want to ask him some questions. As his parent, you have a right to be with him. However, he has asked that I go with him instead."

Judy looked at her carefully. "I trust you, Jan. You seem to know how to reach him. I heard him laughing when he was talking with you. That was nice to hear. Just please tell me if there's anything I should know or do."

"Of course. He just needs some space and time. I'll tell you everything that was asked and said. Thanks."

"Thank you." She went back to her husband and started speaking quietly to him.

Jan went into the kitchen and got Brad, leading him into the family room. When they got there, Sheriff Nolan was writing in a notebook. After a moment, he looked up. "Hi, Ms. Jan, Brad. Brad, everyone calls me Sheriff Ray. My dad was Sheriff Bob and I'm Sheriff Ray."

"Your dad was a cop, too?" Brad asked.

"Yep. A family business. Do you watch cop shows on TV, Brad?"

Brad sat beside Jan on the couch. "Sure."

"Well, don't believe what you see. They make it look like policing is all about fast car chases, gunfights, interrogating criminals. I'll tell you what policing is all about. Paperwork." He held up his notebook. "I've been at this job for over thirty years and I have a garage full of these notebooks, not to mention all the boxes and crates of reports. This, my son, is policing. So I need your help to fill yet another notebook. I'm just going to ask you some questions and I want you to answer as best you can. This isn't a test, like Ms. Jan would give you," he grinned. "There are no wrong answers here. Okay?"

"Okay."

"Just tell me about what you found on the beach. You were going down for a swim, weren't you?"

"More just to stick my feet in the water. I had just had breakfast and there wasn't anyone else on the beach." He stopped. "At least, there wasn't supposed to be anyone else on the beach."

"Okay, I got the picture. So what did you see first?"

"Kitty Jr. was sitting on the beach."

"Kitty Jr.?"

"Elusive Cat's baby," Jan explained.

"Ah, so we have another generation. Continue," Sheriff Ray said.

"He ran when he saw me, of course. He always does. When I looked back at the beach from watching him run behind the house, I could see that there was something on the beach."

"Did you think it was a person?"

"I guess. Looked like someone sleeping. I didn't want to disturb him so I headed a bit over." Brad waved his right arm a bit, indicating which way he'd gone. "But the beach isn't too wide here. So I looked at him as I passed and I saw his eyes." He looked at Jan.

She leaned towards him. "It's okay, Brad. Just tell Sheriff Ray what you saw."

Brad kept his eyes on her as he said, "His eyes were full of sand." His voice shook.

"Did you notice the rest of his face?" Ray asked.

Brad looked at him. "What?"

"Did you see his nose or his mouth? Did they have sand on them?"

"He was lying on his stomach, his head turned. I didn't notice his nose. His mouth was open and there was sand on his lips."

"Doing just fine, Brad. Could you tell if the sand was wet or dry?"

"Looked dry to me, sort of light-colored, not dark as it gets when wet."

"What was he wearing? Did you notice?"

"Not then. The eyes freaked me out a bit. I mean, how could someone have their eyes open and full of sand? That would hurt."

Ray looked at him. "But now you know that it didn't hurt because he couldn't feel it, right?"

"Because he's dead."

"That's right, Brad. He's dead so he doesn't have any pain. The sand went in his eyes after he was dead. It didn't hurt him. Do you understand?"

"Sure."

"Okay, just a few more questions. What did you do when you realized that he was dead?"

"I ran back to the house to get my dad. Then everyone came down to the beach."

"Who was everyone?"

Brad counted them off on his fingers. "Mr. and Mrs. Traeger, my mom and dad and sister, Ms. Lois and Jan. I think that's everyone. Oh, and I saw Cat and Kitty Jr. watching from the side of the house."

"Cats and their curiosity," Ray smiled. "Thank you, Brad. You did that perfectly. Could you ask your sister to come in next? She can bring your mom or dad with her or Ms. Jan can stay."

"Sure, can I keep unloading the dishes?" he asked Jan.

"You sure can and when you finish that, I'm sure Ms. Lois will have other work for you to do. She keeps me busy all the time." He grinned at her and went out.

Jan looked at Sheriff Ray when they were alone. "Why did you want to know about his face?"

Ray looked at her sharply. "Just checking to see how good his powers of observation were. No other reason."

Jan thought a moment. "But if his lips were dry, then there was no water in his mouth. Are you saying that he didn't drown?"

"I'm not saying anything and I would suggest you keep your speculations to yourself, Ms. Cathcart."

27

She pulled back at the official tone in his voice but she couldn't say anything more since Josie appeared at the door. She watched him closely as he turned to the teenager.

"Josie, please have a seat. I just have a few questions."

Chapter 2

Josie could add very little to what Brad had said and Jan, when it was her turn, could add even less. After they were done, she went back into the kitchen while the other guests were called into the family room one at a time. The whole kitchen smelled like rising yeast. Lois had punched the loaves down once and they were doing their final rise before going in the oven.

She had started the kids baking cookies. As far as Jan could see, Brad was working on brownies while Josie was making some chocolate chip. A fair bit of the batter for each wasn't making it into the final product but the kids were having fun. Jan resigned herself to cleaning up the mess after everyone was done. Several of the guests had moved on to tea but she still made another pot of coffee, to keep it fresh. The constable who had been posted on the beach came to the house to speak with the sheriff and snagged a fresh cup for himself before leaving again.

It took a long time for everyone to be questioned. Although Jan didn't think the sheriff would have gotten much useful information. After all, everyone had been here eating breakfast, except Lolinda, who had been sleeping. She wondered if they had found anything in Mr. Ellersby's room. Like a suicide note or something.

Then she realized that he probably had a family somewhere who needed to be told.

Her thoughts were interrupted by Sheriff Ray coming out of the family room with his last guest, Ms. Lolinda. He asked for everyone's attention. Jan, Lois and the kids leaned over the breakfast bar to listen.

"Thank you all so much for your cooperation. We are finished for now. Feel free to continue with your interrupted plans, just please leave a cell phone number where you can be reached if we need to. Ms Lois says that no one is scheduled to check out until Sunday, so I would appreciate it if you would all just stick to that schedule and stay here for the next few days. We have cordoned off a small part of the beach but you can still access the water. Please stay off the cordoned section." He looked at Brad as he said this and Brad nodded.

After he had left with his constables, they all headed for the beach. No one said anything. They just walked silently towards the yellow police tape. But there was nothing to see. The whole area had been swept clean. Jan didn't understand the need for the tape but then she didn't know anything about police investigations. She shrugged her shoulders and checked on Brad. He seemed to be losing interest in the site, too.

Lois must have sensed the awkwardness of the group. "There's fresh bread just about out of the oven. And our two junior assistants have made cookies."

Mr. Tipton spoke up. "How about I run into town and pick up a selection of meat and cheeses to go with that?"

"I'll come with you, Dad," Brad said.

Lois smiled at them. "Thanks. That sounds like a plan. Lunch should be ready in about half an hour or so. Join us if you like or get started on your days. You all heard the sheriff. We can keep to our regular routine while they take care of poor Mr. Ellersby."

Lolinda asked, "Does anyone know if he has any family?"

There was a lot of head shaking. "The police will find that out," Lois replied. "I'll pass along any information that I get. Jan, shall we get started on that cleaning that we had planned?"

Josie came over to Jan. "Can I help?"

"You like to clean?!"

Josie grinned. "Actually, I do!"

"When we all get back to the Bay Area, you can visit me any time!" Jan laughed.

Everyone else did, too. The group scattered after that. Jan looked back to see Judy Tipton still standing beside the cordoned-off square of sand. She said to Lois and Josie, "I'll be with you guys in a minute."

Judy looked up as she stood beside her. Jan just said quietly, "Brad's going be okay. He's a strong kid and you have given him a good foundation. Just let him have some time and listen if he wants to talk. That's all we can do for kids. I would say don't worry, but I know that's not possible." She smiled. "You could help us clean but you're on vacation. Perhaps you wouldn't mind setting out the fixings for lunch. It does help to have something to do. Your kids seem to know that."

"Thanks, Jan. And for everything you're doing for the kids. I can certainly help with lunch. After all, this is a bed and breakfast, not bed and lunch. I'll be glad to help you and your sister."

They walked back to the house and Lois got Judy started in the kitchen. Jan explained the spiderweb hunt to Josie and they headed off with dust cloths and long-handled brooms. Soon enough the car was back with sandwich stuffers. People gathered around, informally mixing, while making sandwiches. The Tiptons discussed the kayak expedition, with Herr Traeger listening in. Frau Traeger and Lolinda sat together talking about jewelry, from what Jan overheard. It seemed the event that morning had broken down the barriers between family groups.

Everyone carried their own dishes to the kitchen with Brad supervising the loading of the dishwasher. The afternoon plans were finalized. Jan would take the Tiptons and Herr Traeger to the kayak booth. The two older women would take a car into the town for some shopping. Josie seemed undecided between the two expeditions but ended up going kayaking. Jan walked them all along the beach, around the point which separated the B&B from the row of rental cottages lining the beach further south. Mixed in among the cottages were various vendors, including one that hired out seagoing kayaks by the hour. She left them there and wandered back.

As she approached within sight of the house, she saw a gray shape within the police tape. She walked over slowly as Kitty Jr. kept a close eye on her. Jan stopped several feet away and crouched down to make herself less intimidating. "You're not supposed to be there. Didn't you hear the sheriff? You could get in trouble."

The small cat just looked at her for a moment and then skittered off towards the house. Jan smiled and followed.

33

Inside, she found Lois sitting at the small kitchen table with a cup of coffee. Jan got one for herself and joined her sister. She also brought over a plate of cookies.

"Everyone is taken care of for the rest of the day," she said. "Good thing you made all those loaves. There's not much left."

Lois nodded absently. "I'll put what's left out for breakfast tomorrow."

"The kids did a good job with these cookies." Jan ate one, watching her sister. She could guess what was bothering her sister but she would let Lois have time to say it herself.

"Yeah." Lois took a sip. "Thanks for helping out. Those kids seem to like you. Guess that's because of your job."

Jan gave a small smile. "You might say that but actually I do my job because I like the kids, not the other way around. Kids are so transparent and honest. Not like us adults."

At this statement, Lois looked at her. "That's for sure."

Jan sighed. She had opened that door. She owed her sister something for her accommodations, in more ways than one. "I know that I've been anything but transparent and honest, Lois. Something really terrible happened and I'm struggling to deal with it. I really appreciate the time and space that you've given me. It's been a big help."

"You know I could help more if I had more details," Lois spoke carefully.

"Maybe someday, when I'm ready. But we've had enough to deal with today."

Lois looked back down into her coffee cup. "It may not be over."

"What do you mean?"

"Jan, someone who was my guest died here today!"

"But it wasn't your fault!"

"It may not matter. Once the news gets out, I could be finished. No one is going to want to stay at a place where people die."

"That's an exaggeration! Don't make this into a drama, Lois. Your current guests are staying," Jan pointed out.

"Because the sheriff told them to. Otherwise, they'd be heading for the door."

"You don't know that. We need to wait until the police tell us the cause of death. For all we know, they may have found a suicide note in his bedroom. Or he may just have swum out too far and drowned from exhaustion."

"He still died here," Lois insisted.

"Everyone has to die somewhere and we can't all manage it quietly at home or in a hospital. Accidents and suicides happen all over. There is no way that blame can be attached to you or your B&B. I think you're worrying about nothing. You'll see."

Lois stood up, taking her cup to the sink to rinse. "I hope you're right. Anyways, I have some phone calls to make. I've lost a whole morning with this."

"Phone calls?"

"Yes, people inquiring for rooms."

"See, it will be fine," Jan said. "I'll keep cleaning. I'll start in the guest house so I don't disturb you."

"Okay." Lois went into her bedroom/office on the main floor and closed the door.

Jan covered the cookies with plastic wrap and set them out for others to nibble on. She did a quick check of the kitchen and then headed to the guest house with supplies for cleaning the bathroom.

As she scrubbed and wiped, she kept thinking about the sheriff's question about the mouth. And Brad's reply. The sand had been dry. And she didn't remember whether the sand under his head had been wet. In fact, he had looked crumpled. Like he'd been wet and had started to dry off. But he hadn't been at the edge of the water. He had been further up. If he had drowned, should he have been that far up on the beach? But if he hadn't drowned, how had he died? Sat down on the sand and had a heart attack. That could happen but he had seemed healthy and fit.

She decided she would watch the tide more closely to see if it ever came up that high, so as to deposit the body up there. She hoped it would all be resolved nice and neatly. But life was rarely nice and neat. She stopped cleaning the back of the toilet as she realized that she hadn't thought about Greg or the conversation for the whole morning. At least she could thank Mr. Ellersby for that, she thought sarcastically.

After cleaning, she felt hot and grubby so she went for a long swim out to the buoy. As she clung there, getting her breath back for the swim to shore, she thought about Brad. She hoped his memory of those eyes would be buried by more pleasant memories of kayaking. With a renewed push not to let her strength vanish with age, she pushed off the buoy and swam out strongly for the beach. It was a long swim and her burst of youthful energy deserted her a long way out. She was gasping as she lay in the shallows, not sure her shaking legs would let her stand. So much for being in the same condition she had been twenty years ago. She would have to work at it if she didn't want to lose it all. She vowed to swim each day, resting for shorter periods on the buoy. Maybe one day she would make it there and back in one go.

She heard voices coming along the beach and decided that she really didn't want to be found sprawled on the sand. She pushed her way to her feet as the kayakers returned. They were all talking and laughing as Brad described some daring move with his hands. They went to the house to change for dinner.

Lolinda and Frau Traeger had returned an hour earlier. The German lady had had several bags from a variety of stores. Jan briefly thought about warning her husband but then figured that he probably knew his wife well enough. He wouldn't be surprised. She headed back to her own room and thought about her own dinner. She doubted that Lois would be in the mood to cook anything that evening.

Her dinner problem was solved as she opened the front door of the guest house. Lolinda had left her own door open and came to it when she heard Jan enter. She invited Jan to join her for dinner in the town at a little, but good quality, seafood restaurant. Jan accepted with pleasure and went to change.

Dinner was spent mostly talking about their careers. They talked a bit about their childhoods. Lolinda had been born and raised in New York City. Broadway had been her dream for her whole life. She'd had her first bit part at age fourteen and had never looked back. Jan had skimmed over a normal life in the Midwest and her decision to move to California. Then she had asked questions about the theater. Lolinda had shared inner secrets and stories for all of the main course. While sitting through tea, she had asked Jan about her job and the rest of the evening was filled with stories of various students and their antics. It was a wonderful evening and the shadow of Mr. Ellersby only intruded during the drive home.

As she weaved the car slowly through the tiny side streets that made up the town of Henry's Harbor, Lolinda said, "You know, I had an interesting conversation with Matt Ellersby a couple of evenings ago. Everyone else had already gone to bed and I was sitting in the breakfast room enjoying a last cup of tea. He came in from dinner, I guess. At first I don't think he saw me. He went and got a cup of coffee. Then as he turned to find somewhere to sit, he saw me. I asked him to join me. He hesitated but then came and sat at the table."

"What did you talk about?" Jan asked.

"At first, nothing. We just sat. But it wasn't uncomfortable. Then he said that he'd heard I was an actress. I told him I was. He asked whether or not I ever got my roles mixed up with my reality."

Jan looked at her sharply. "That's an interesting question."

"I thought so, too. I said that my roles were my job and I tried not to take them home. Not that I always succeed, especially with some of the more disturbing ones. But I try."

"What did he say?"

"He was silent for a moment and then he said that he guessed that everyone actually played roles most of their lives. I asked what he meant and he said roles like son, husband, father and those. But I think he meant something else."

"What do you mean? Why did you think that?"

"Just the way he said it. I'm pretty good at reading people. I need to be able to reproduce all kinds of emotions, even if I have never felt them myself. So I've become a studier of people. His body and eyes weren't aligning with what his mouth was saying. He was talking about a deeper kind of role. Like when a person pretends to be something that they're not."

"In what way?"

"You've met them. The people who pretend to be generous but are skinflints at heart. Or the ones who claim to be interested in you but actually have their own agenda."

Jan nodded. "I know the type very well," she sighed, thinking of Greg and his 'agenda.' "What do you think he was hiding?"

"I have no idea. He got up and left after that. And now he has taken his secrets to the grave."

"Unless the police uncover something, you're probably right. I never really had a chance to talk with him. He seemed to put up boundaries."

Lolinda took her eyes off the road for a moment and looked at Jan with a slight smile. "Just like you."

Jan was startled. Then she gave a crooked smile. "We all have our secrets, I guess. I'll try not to be so unapproachable in the future. Thank you for inviting me to dinner. I really enjoyed it."

"I figured I could give you a break from washing pots," Lolinda said.

Jan laughed. "Honestly, I don't do that much. Just in the morning when you all are in the breakfast room. The rest of the day is pretty much my own."

"I can see that. So you chose to spend your day cleaning our bathroom?" Another smile.

"Not really. But I do owe my sister a fair bit. She's not charging me rent so I pay with helping out."

"Sort of like indentured servitude?"

Jan laughed a lot over that. It was such a silly comment and Lolinda delivered it perfectly. They went to their separate rooms, both still smiling.

Maybe it was the big meal. Or maybe it was the day's events. But Jan found herself awake at about 2:00 a.m. She tried to read a bit but couldn't focus. So she silently got up and pulled some sweat pants over her pajamas. She grabbed a sweatshirt from the pile and quietly went out to the beach. There was a half moon, which shone lightly on the waves. She sat on the sand, which was still warm from the day's heat. She slipped her sandals off and tucked her feet under her legs. Then she tried to focus on the endless rhythm of the water coming in and going back out. It should have been soothing but she just couldn't get in tune with it.

Then she realized that she wasn't alone. The small gray kitten was sitting about five feet away from her, also staring at the water. "It's past your bedtime, little one," she said softly.

The kitten looked at her and then went back to staring at the waves. Jan copied him. "Not working for me tonight. Too many bad vibes out here. Or maybe inside me. Three months - you would think I could move past it in three months. It was the right decision. Maybe not handled in the best way but the right decision." She looked at her companion who turned his attention from the water to return her gaze. "I mean, if you consider his reaction, that just proves my point. He said he loved me and yet, like that." She snapped her fingers but the cat didn't react. "Just like that he says that I'm garbage. That I've wasted his time. That I am a terrible person. You don't say things like that to someone you love." Her voice was rising. "You don't say things like that to anyone."

The cat let out a tiny meow. Jan instantly stopped talking. "Sorry for yelling. I guess I'm still mad. At him or at myself? That's the issue. Maybe I should have clued in years ago. Maybe I did waste his time. But he said that he loved me. And I loved him. At least the 'him' that I thought he was. And that I guess was the problem. We were playing roles in order to get what we wanted and we just didn't want the same thing. Still, I don't think his telling everyone that I was a cold-hearted b... Well you know what I mean. That was just brutal. Especially for the kids. I had to leave. Can't you see that? I just had to leave."

The kitten turned back to the waves and curled up in the sand. Jan just looked at it. Her eyes filled with tears. "I guess that is the only answer because there is no answer. It's over. Everything I had there is gone. So now I'm here, in Maine, sitting on a beach at two in the morning, talking with a little kitten. And somehow that will just have to do. Mourn and move on." She lay down on the sand and curled up, too, watching both the kitten and the sea. Over the waves, she could hear a soft purring. She let her eyes close.

"Hey! Are you okay?" the voice was high-pitched.

Jan opened her eyes to see the sun rising over the waves. She took a moment to figure out where she was. On the beach. She must have fallen asleep. She sat up, wrapping her arms around herself and then turned to the speaker. Brad was standing about ten feet away staring at her in fright. "It's okay, Brad. I'm fine. I came out here earlier and must have fallen asleep." She looked around. "Did you see Kitty Jr.? He was here, too."

"No, you were alone. I saw you on the beach and I thought...I mean..." He couldn't go on.

Jan got quickly to her feet. "I'm sorry, Brad. I didn't mean to frighten you. I'm fine. You're out early."

"Couldn't sleep," he mumbled.

"Same problem here. Why don't you get your swimsuit and we'll go for an early morning swim? Wash the cobwebs away."

"Sure, be back in a minute."

Jan watched him jog back up the beach as she walked to her room. It must have really given him a scare to see another body on the beach. She would have to talk to him about that. In her room, she looked at the clock and saw that it was nearly 7:00 a.m. Well, she had some sort of sleep. Hopefully enough to get through the rest of the day. In fact, despite the unconventional bed, she felt quite rested. Maybe Kitty Jr. was just the therapy she needed. She grinned at that thought and slipped into her swimsuit, grabbing a towel.

They started out together but quite quickly, Brad pulled ahead. He politely waited at the buoy for her to arrive. She hung on, gasping. "You said you were a good swimmer and you weren't kidding. Look at you! Barely breathing hard and I am panting like a dog."

He grinned. "Actually, you don't swim badly for a...you know what I mean."

"An out-of-shape school teacher?"

He laughed.

"Aw, shucks. Thanks, mister," Jan cracked out. "At least you didn't say 'for a girl.'"

Brad laughed. "Josie is a great swimmer."

"So make me feel really old. Just for that, you can lead the way back!"

He pushed off and raced towards the beach. She was smiling as she followed more slowly. When she got to the beach, he was resting on his towel, building a small sand castle beside him. Jan saw his mother standing at the door of the B&B. She raised her hand in greeting and the woman went back in. Brad turned to look at the house. "Who were you waving at?"

"Your mom. Just making sure you weren't swimming alone."

"I'm not that dumb, you know. She acts like I don't have any brains."

Jan put her towel on the sand near him and sat down. "Are you telling me that everything you do, you think through first? Consider all the consequences?"

He looked down at the castle and didn't answer.

"Exactly," Jan agreed. "You've got a good head on your shoulders and your mom knows it. But you're not an adult yet. That doesn't mean that you don't make good choices a lot of the time. It just means that you don't know everything yet. Her job, and mine too as a teacher, is to make sure you grow up and have a chance to learn it all. So, as I said yesterday, give her a break. She's being a mom and you're being her kid. Which, by the way, you will still be when you are fifty and she is in her seventies. So you'd better get used to it. There are some things in life you can't change. And mothers are one of those. And that ends our lesson for today. I'm hungry so I should probably get in there and help with breakfast. See you there."

When she got to the guest house, she looked back. He was standing up and kicking the castle apart with his foot. But he didn't look angry. Then he headed for the main house. She changed quickly and went to help Lois. "Sorry I'm late. I went for a swim with Brad. He was out there early."

"And you were, too?" Lois asked carefully.

Jan smiled. "I was talking with Kitty Jr. He's a good listener. Now, I'll go set the tables. Sorry again for being late."

Her sister was still staring at her as she went through the door. She knew that soon she would have to give Lois at least the bare basics of what had happened. The guests started coming down and the day seemed to be progressing as usual. Lois had made a vegetable-filled omelet and waffles today. Brad whooped in joy when he saw the waffles. Jan counted at least six on his plate. Everyone laughed.

It seemed that Frau Traeger had gotten her fill of shopping the day before because they quickly decided on a day in Acadia National Park. Lois told them of a sandwich place in town that would fix up a picnic lunch for them. They were soon gone. The Tiptons went on a scheduled fishing expedition. Soon the house was quiet again. Lois started working in her office and Jan finished cleaning up the kitchen. She put away the leftover waffles. She knew from experience that Lolinda would have some of the omelet.

As she was drying the last frying pan, there was a knock at the door. When Lois didn't come out, she went and answered it. Sheriff Ray stood there. "Morning, Jan. Could I speak with your sister?"

"Sure, come on in. I'll just get her. Help yourself to a cup of coffee."

He moved towards the pot while she went and knocked on Lois' door. "Sheriff Ray is here. Wants to talk with you."

"Okay, coming."

Ray was seated at one of the round tables. He indicated a chair on the other side. "Grab a seat, Lois. I've got some disturbing news."

Lois sat down slowly. Jan brought her a fresh cup of coffee and then went into the kitchen, where she could still hear their voices but not interfere. "What is it, Ray? About Mr. Ellersby?"

"Yes, he didn't drown. There was no water in his lungs. His clothes showed that he had been in the water but he didn't die there. More likely he was already dead and the high tide soaked him."

"Then how did he die? Heart attack or stroke?"

"No, he was poisoned. And the only thing in his stomach, besides the poison, was some sort of dessert thing with chocolate and coconut, as far as we can tell. It was barely digested."

"Oh, no." Lois put her hand to her mouth.

Jan could still picture the little plate of petit fours that Lois had saved for Mr. Ellersby to eat when he got back from dinner.

Chapter 3

"What is it?" Ray asked.

"It can't be," Lois mumbled.

"What can't be?"

"There wasn't any poison. They were just petit fours."

"What's a petit four?"

Lois finally looked at him but the color had not yet returned to her face. "A petit four is a small pastry." She held her hand up to show the size. "I made them that afternoon as a treat for everyone. Actually, it was a dare to myself. They are not easy to make, not well. I made four different kinds: chocolate, raspberry, coconut, and caramel. Everyone ate them."

"Including Matthew Ellersby?"

"He wasn't here in the evening when I served them with coffee. He never came back until later. But I saved him some. Otherwise, Brad would have eaten all of them." There was a slight smile, quickly gone.

"So you set some aside for Mr. Ellersby. Where did you put them?"

"I covered the plate with plastic wrap and left them on the counter," she pointed towards it. "Then I put a little sign on it with his name so that he would know they were for him."

"And they were gone in the morning?"

Lois thought for a moment. "Yes, and the plate was in the sink."

"Where's the plate now?"

"Went into the dishwasher and was washed with yesterday's breakfast dishes."

"A pity."

"But there was no poison in them!" Lois exclaimed. "We all ate them and are fine."

"It could have been added later. That plate would have sat there all evening. Anyone could have added anything. The plate might have had a remnant of the poison. Well, that's gone now." He stood up. "I'll have to ask you to come to the station for some more questioning."

Lois looked up in fear. "But I haven't done anything!"

"I'm not saying that you have. But those little desserts are the only clue that we have. And you made them. So, please, come with me."

"But I can't leave here. The guests! What if someone needs something?"

"This is a bed and breakfast, and breakfast is done. You need to come now."

Jan stepped out of the kitchen and went to Lois. "It's okay. I'll stay here to answer the phone and deal with any issues with the guests. You won't be gone long. Will she, Sheriff?"

"We'll see," Sheriff Ray said. "Let's go."

He led Lois out. She went quietly, looking back over her shoulder at Jan who tried to smile confidently. Then the house was quiet. Jan suddenly felt like a cup of coffee. And maybe a few of those cookies. She took them into Lois' office/bedroom. She had only seen the room from the doorway. It had probably been some sort of back parlor. Lois had converted it into a cozy bedroom with a desk and filing cabinets. Jan sat down at the desk with her coffee.

This was getting to be a mess. There was no way Lois had poisoned those petit fours but she couldn't imagine anyone else doing it. Maybe it still was suicide and Ellersby had taken the poison after eating the treats. That seemed the most reasonable answer.

She tried to remember that afternoon. The days here followed a pattern so it was hard to distinguish them. Except for the petit fours. Once the breakfast dishes had been cleared and some office work taken care of, Lois had retreated to the kitchen. Jan had heard her mumbling to herself and stayed out of the way. She had gone for a swim and then met Lolinda coming out of her room on her way to her late breakfast. Jan had gone with her to heat up her breakfast and make fresh coffee. Lois hadn't even looked up from her recipe book when Jan had used the microwave.

Making sure that the actress had everything she needed, Jan had again left to go for a walk along the beach. She had wished for the hundredth time that Lois had a kayak she could just take out. But Lois wouldn't have anything to do with boats. Not since John's death on a deep sea expedition. Guests had to walk to the next beach and rent whatever watercraft they wanted. Jan toyed with the idea of looking around for a used kayak that she could buy. But that depended on how long she intended to stay in Maine. That speculation had, as usual, gone nowhere. She had wandered back in time to see the Tiptons coming back from their day's adventure. They had all gone in to taste the petit fours. They had been wonderful.

Jan remembered thinking that Lois had spent all day on those and they had vanished in a flash. She shook her head again at the illogic of it all. She would never understand cooks. She gave a slight smile. But she would enjoy their efforts. And those petit fours had been some of the best that she had ever tasted. Lois had received their delighted praise with a happy smile. And now those same little tasty tidbits were mixed with poison in a corpse's body in the morgue. A depressing thought. Joy and delight were so short-lived. Jan left the office. She would sit in the eating room. She could still hear the phone and it was less filled with Lois' worrying presence.

She looked out the front window and saw the kitten again inside the police lines. Perhaps he smelled something that the police had left. Perhaps he was just curious. The day passed slowly. Jan made herself a sandwich from the leftovers of the day before. She answered the phone a few times and took messages. None of the guests arrived until nearly 5:00 p.m. Then the Tiptons came to take a quick swim and change for dinner. Brad and Josie waved at her as they came past. She watched them swim for a bit and then straightened as she saw Sheriff Ray coming around the house from the road. She didn't see Lois with him. She went to the door.

Ray was raising his hand to knock when she opened it. He lowered his hand. "Jan," he acknowledged. "Your sister said that Mr. Ellersby arrived with two suitcases. Can you verify that?"

"Sorry, I wasn't here when he arrived. What's the problem? Where's Lois?"

"My constables searched and cleared his room but found only one suitcase. I'd like to look in his room again."

"Certainly," Jan said. "I'll take you up."

"I know the way."

Jan followed him to the base of the stairs. She could hear him moving around up there. Then as he headed back for the stairs, the door opened and the Tiptons came in, hair dripping and towels wrapped around themselves. They stopped as they saw Jan at the bottom of the stairs.

"What's up?" Brad asked.

"The sheriff just wanted to check something upstairs," Jan answered as the man in question started coming back down. "Did you find it?"

"Find what?" Brad asked.

"Brad!" his mother said. "Don't be so nosy!"

"That's okay, Mrs. Tipton. I'm hoping maybe one of you might be able to help me. Ms. Lois said that Mr. Ellersby had two suitcases when he arrived. Did any of you see him arrive and can confirm that?"

"Sure," Mr. Tipton said. "We were all sitting here trying to decide what to have for dinner. It was late afternoon. He definitely had two suitcases. A big one and a slightly smaller one."

"Well, there was only one up there yesterday. Did anyone see him take the other out with him at any time?"

The family all looked at each other. Jan shook her head. "He often came down for breakfast after everyone else had left so they wouldn't have seen anything. I was still in the kitchen most mornings helping with the clean-up and I certainly never saw him carrying a suitcase. Of course, he might have taken it out later in the day. There's often no one right here in this room during the day."

"Or he might have just put it in the secret cubbyhole," Brad said.

"The secret cubbyhole?" Ray stared at him. "What do you mean, young man?"

"The closets have secret cubbyholes. At least ours does and my parents' room. I thought they might all have one."

Ray looked at Jan. "Did you know about these?"

"Never heard of them. How did you find yours, Brad?" Jan asked the boy.

"I was looking for my baseball cap. Couldn't find it and thought I might have tossed it at the back of the top shelf in the closet. I couldn't reach back there so I got the chair from the desk and put it in there. To stand on, you know. But when I put the chair down, the floor sounded sort of hollow. So I moved the chair and checked out the floor. If you look carefully, you can see the door. I pried it up with my pocket knife and found a good-sized cubbyhole there. I went into my parents' room and found another one there. Ms. Lois said that they had been built during Prohibition to store the smuggled whiskey. I thought that was sort of cool."

"You all wait here and I will check the room."

"Sheriff," Judy spoke up. "Could we at least get changed? We're dripping all over Lois' floor."

He looked at them and then nodded. "But I would ask you all to come straight down here again."

They nodded and followed him up the stairs. Jan went into the kitchen. Looked like coffee and maybe lemonade would be needed. She also put out the rest of the cookies. It wasn't long before the sheriff came downstairs with a suitcase in a large plastic bag. The Tiptons were following him. At the bottom, the sheriff turned to Brad. "Thank you for your suggestion, young man. Do you have any idea how Mr. Ellersby might have known about the storage space?"

"He may have heard me asking Ms. Lois about it. There were some people around but I can't remember who."

"I'll ask Ms. Lois."

"When is she coming back?" Jan asked.

"If you would like to come to the station in about an hour, you will be able to pick her up." The sheriff went out the door with his evidence. The Tiptons left for dinner. Jan decided to find a place in town that made takeout dinners. Lois wouldn't want to cook and she wouldn't want to inflict her own cooking on her sister.

She had just pulled out the phone book when the Traegers arrived.

Herr Traeger said, "We passed the sheriff as we came in. Is Ms. Lois back?"

"I'll be going to pick her up soon. Just figuring out dinner." Jan indicated the book.

"Then why was he here?" Frau Traeger asked. "Is everything okay?"

"I don't know. He came back to look for Mr. Ellersby's second suitcase."

"Did he find it?"

"Yes. Did either of you know about the hidden storage spaces in the closets?"

Herr Traeger nodded. "I heard the Tipton boy discussing it with Ms. Lois. She was telling him about the smugglers."

"I don't remember that," his wife said.

"I don't think you were here, mein lieber."

"I didn't know anything about these spaces. In the closets?"

"Yes, Brad found one in his room and, according to him, there's one in all the closets."

"We'll have to check ours but we do need to get changed for dinner. We have that reservation," Frau Traeger said to her husband. Then she turned back to Jan. "Someone recommended this good seafood restaurant - The Wandering Albatross."

Jan nodded. "I went there yesterday with Ms. Lolinda. It is very good. Enjoy your evening."

"Danke." They went upstairs and Jan got to work on the phone.

By 6:30 p.m., she was at the police station with their dinner wrapped in two bags in the back seat. She only had to wait a few minutes until her sister was escorted through an inner door. Lois just looked at her and walked to the front door. Jan followed and then led her to the car. As she drove off, she looked at her sister sideways. Lois looked stretched and thin. "Must have been a rough day," Jan said quietly. "I picked up some dinner. Figured it was safer than my cooking."

Lois just stared out the window so Jan didn't make any other attempts at conversation. When they got to the B&B, Lois got out of the car and went silently into her bedroom. Jan got out plates and silverware and set the small table for them. The rest of the house was silent. She went to Lois' door and heard the shower running. She put the dinner in the oven on low to keep it warm. Then she sat at the front window and watched the ocean for a bit. She had just decided to go to her room and get a book to read when Lois' door opened. She seemed surprised to see Jan waiting. But she followed her into the kitchen and sat at the table while Jan got the food and uncovered it. Jan had opted for Chinese. It wouldn't be too heavy and made for good leftovers if they didn't eat much. She herself was quite hungry but she didn't know if Lois would eat.

She served herself and then waited until Lois slowly picked up the serving spoon and ladled some chicken and vegetables onto her plate. They ate silently. Jan helped herself to seconds and was pleased when she saw Lois do the same. They still hadn't spoken a word when they finished. Jan picked up the plates and rinsed them, then put them in the dishwasher. She collected the leftover food and combined it into one container, which she put in the fridge. Lois didn't look at her once, staring at something in her mind. When Jan had finished, she sat back down and waited again.

Finally, Lois looked up at her. "Thanks for that and everything," she said, indicating the house.

"Not a problem."

"It doesn't seem real. I spent the whole day sitting in this empty room, which smelled of stale coffee and cigarette smoke. Sometimes Ray came in to ask me questions but mostly I sat."

"They just made you wait?! Did they at least feed you lunch?"

"Some totally flavorless sandwiches. I don't even know what they were supposed to be. And their coffee is terrible."

"Maybe you could start a side business supplying the police station with food and coffee?" Jan said, smiling.

Lois did smile at that. Then her eyes filled with tears. "Oh, Jan. What am I going to do? They just kept asking me about poor Mr. Ellersby. Why might he have wanted to harm himself? Why might I have wanted to kill him? Me?! What are they thinking?! I hardly knew the man. He seemed decent enough but he never really talked to me. How could I answer those questions? And then, when they found the suitcase, there were more questions.

Why had he hidden it there? Had I told him about the space myself?"

Jan interjected, "But he knew that Brad had been the one to find the cubbyholes. I didn't even know about them. But Brad said that you did?"

Lois nodded. "I found them when we were renovating the place after we bought it. I asked around and found that Maine had a healthy smuggling business during Prohibition. Actually long before that because Maine was dry before the rest of the country. Most of the houses built around that time have storage spaces for whiskey. I don't keep it a secret but I don't usually tell guests about them either because I don't want to have to check them for left-behind luggage all the time. But Brad found the one in his closet and then the one in his parents' room. So I told him. And, as I told Ray, several other guests were around at the time. I can't remember specifically if Mr. Ellersby was there or not but he could have been."

"Did Ray tell you what was in the suitcase that may have made Mr. Ellersby hide it?"

"One thing I learned today, Jan, is that the police never tell you anything. It is a one-way street. They ask and we answer. It doesn't work the other way. They never once answered any of my questions. And they're not done yet."

"What do you mean?"

"Ray said they would be back tomorrow morning. He wanted to know what time we serve breakfast."

"He's tired of the station food?"

"I think he wants to catch all the guests together. He's going to drive them away. He's going to kill this place."

Jan stood up and put a hand on her sister's shoulder. "You're exhausted, Lois. Go to bed. I'll be here early and we can make breakfast together. You boss and I'll do. We'll get through this, you'll see. You have a great place and a good reputation. This will all fade into history soon enough."

Lois stood up. "I hope you're right, Jan, but somehow I don't think so. Thanks for your help. I really appreciate it."

"It's what sisters are for," Jan said simply.

Lois nodded and gave her a brief hug before going to her own room. Jan quickly got her book and returned to read in the family room until all the guests had returned from dinner. None of them wanted to stay down and socialize or play games. They just went straight to their rooms. She locked everything up and went back to her place. She had heard nothing from Lois.

Whether it was because the day's events pushed her own thoughts to the background or because of her late-night therapy session with Kitty Jr., Jan slept peacefully through the night. She awoke around 6:00 and dressed quickly. The house was still quiet except for a light on in the kitchen. She found Lois working on some muffins. It didn't look like Lois had shared her peaceful night. "What can I do?" she asked quietly.

"We'll need chopped mushrooms, onions, the little green ones, red pepper and spinach. I'm making quiche this morning."

"Okay." Jan got the vegetables out of the refrigerator, washed them and started chopping them into tiny pieces. They worked silently. When she had finished that and had partially cooked chopped bacon in the frying pan, she started work on the coffee. Lois put the ingredients together in several quiche pans and put them in the oven. By then, the muffins were out and filling the kitchen with the lovely smell of cinnamon and apple. With the coffee brewing, Jan set tables and put out the juices. She could hear movements from upstairs and shortly the guests came down. They seemed a bit subdued but greeted Lois with genuine warmth. As usual, they ate lots and praised the chef.

Lois thanked them but kept looking at the door. Jan had been checking it herself for the last half hour. If the sheriff didn't come soon, all the guests would be gone and there wouldn't be much breakfast left. Just as it looked like he had indeed left it too late, he came around the side of the house. Jan wondered whether or not he had been waiting until they had all finished eating. She hadn't seen him peeking in but he might have, or sent one of his constables. There was one with him now. The same one as on the day of the body discovery.

Jan opened the door for them while Lois retreated to the kitchen. Sheriff Ray greeted everyone pleasantly and both he and his constable accepted Jan's offer of coffee. Then he stood by the breakfast bar. His constable stayed near the front door but had his notepad out ready.

"I won't take much of your time, ladies and gentlemen. We just have a few more questions about Mr. Ellersby. Did any of you speak with him?"

Herr Traeger spoke up. "He asked me once about Germany. I was down here waiting for my wife and he came down. I thought he was just going to go out but then he came over and asked if he could sit with me while he drank his coffee. Of course I said yes."

"What did he want to know?"

"Just some general questions about life in Germany. He commented that he had never been there but had always wanted to go. He said that he might go there soon."

"Interesting. Anything else."

The German thought for a moment. "I asked what he wanted to visit or see but he didn't seem to have any idea. Then he asked how easy it was to immigrate to Germany. I told him I had no clue."

"Very interesting," Ray said. "And anything more?"

"No, my wife came down. He stood up, nodded to her, put his cup on the counter and left. I never spoke to him again."

"And Mrs. Traeger? Did he speak with you?"

"No, Sheriff. Nothing more than a brief hello if we passed."

"Anyone else?"

They all shook their heads. Jan said, "He never joined the others for breakfast or evening coffee. I have no idea where he went during the day but he was never here. Why, Sheriff Ray? Why do you want to know if he spoke with us?"

"I was hoping that he might have mentioned what he was doing here. We found a suitcase in his room yesterday. Inside was a driver's license in the name of Ted Marston. His car was also rented in that name. Has anyone ever heard that name before?" He was watching the guests very carefully but there wasn't anything. They just looked back and shook their heads. Herr Traeger's napkin had slipped to the floor and his wife retrieved it but otherwise there was no movement.

"Okay," the sheriff continued. "Please enjoy your day. Thank you for your time."

They all left upstairs to get their things. Shortly after, everyone was out the front door. Jan started to clear the tables. Ray moved over towards the muffins.

"Help yourself," Jan said. Then she looked at the constable still standing by the door. "You, too."

He nodded his thanks and took one, while refreshing his coffee cup. Then he settled at a table by the window. The sheriff stayed leaning against the bar. Lois ignored him and started straightening the kitchen. Jan carried the dishes into the kitchen and rinsed and loaded them in the dishwasher. The sheriff just kept munching and watching. Jan found it disturbing and then realized that he was probably doing it for that purpose. She looked over at her sister and saw that Lois had gone pale again. She went over to her, ostensibly to get a pot near her, and put a comforting hand on her arm. "Take a deep breath, Lois. You've done nothing wrong. Just remember that. You've done nothing wrong."

Lois gave her a half smile. Then she walked over to the counter. "Is there something more you want, Ray?"

"I was just wondering. When he registered, did you take a look at his driver's license?"

"No," she answered firmly. "He paid cash, well, traveler's checks, which is the same thing, for a week. He said his plans were still unknown and wanted to know if he might be able to stay longer. I told him that I would warn him before the last room booked up for next week. He thanked me, signed the register and that was that."

"Why didn't you ask to see his driver's license?"

"What did it matter? If he wanted to register under another name, what's it to me? They could all be using aliases, for all I know. As long as they pay and follow the rules, it's not my business."

"Most hosts take driver's license numbers," he commented.

"I'm not most hosts. I respect people's privacy. I offer a bed and a breakfast. That's all. I'm not the police." She said the last with a touch of bitterness.

Ray looked at her sharply but didn't say anything for a moment. Then he changed the subject. "How long have you known about the secret cubbies?"

"Since I bought the place. I don't tell guests but Brad discovered them. I don't hide them but, as I told Jan, I don't need more places for guests to forget things. I also don't need more spaces to clean."

"So you never learned anything more about him?"

"I already told you that. Whatever his name was, I don't know anything about him. He was just a guest who needed a room. A quiet guest who caused no trouble."

"Until he died," Jan mumbled. Lois shot her a quick look which showed she had heard. Ray didn't move.

Then he stood up. "Thanks for the muffins and coffee."

Lois just nodded. Jan followed the sheriff to the door and closed it behind the men. She watched them go around the corner of the house and then saw the kitten watching her from the edge of the beach. As she looked, the kitten turned and moved back into the weeds. She went back into the kitchen. "Things keep getting stranger and stranger. I wonder why he was traveling under an assumed name."

"Not you, too?" Lois said.

"What?"

"Can't you leave the wondering to the police? I've had enough of it. I don't care what name he registered under. Why should it matter to me? He could have been on the FBI's Most Wanted list, for all I care. He paid his bill, he didn't bother anyone. He was a model guest."

"Until he died," Jan repeated.

Lois sank into a chair. She put her head in her hands. "Damn. Damn, damn, damn. Why did he have to die here?"

There was no answer to that. Jan finished wiping the last counter. "Is there anything I can help you with today?"

Lois sighed and looked up. "I was going to clean his room but I don't think they've removed the police tape yet. Maybe I'll do some work on the roadside gardens. They're looking a bit ragged."

If there was one thing that Jan hated more than cooking, it was gardening. But she vowed to help her sister if she could. But she couldn't prevent a brief grimace from crossing her face at the thought of it.

Her sister smiled when she looked at her. "Don't worry. I won't make you garden. I remember how you hated it when Mother asked you to help. You were here all day yesterday. You deserve a day off. Go enjoy yourself."

"Are you sure?"

"Yeah, I'll be fine. It will do me good to hack a few weeds. I'll see you at dinner. I believe it's my turn to cook."

Jan grinned. "It's always your turn to cook. If you want to eat, I mean."

Lois was smiling as Jan left. She decided to spend the day in the nearby national forest. Jan loved hiking there. She had missed that in California. The forests there were either too far away or too expensive to explore. But Lois had given her a season's pass to Acadia. So she changed into comfortable hiking clothes. As she was just leaving, Lolinda came out of her room, looking as elegant as ever in a mid-calf-length flowing sundress. Jan had briefly toyed with the idea of telling the sheriff that Lolinda had spoken with the dead man. But she decided to leave that to Lolinda.

The actress looked her up and down. "I see a day of hiking in your future."

Jan grinned. "How perceptive."

"Any more excitement this morning?"

"The sheriff was by asking if anyone had spoken with Mr. Ellersby, who by the way, wasn't Mr. Ellersby."

"He wasn't?"

"No, evidently his name was Ted Marston."

Lolinda thought about that. "Here under a false name? Wonder what he was hiding from. And that explains the time on the beach."

"You mean in the morning?"

"No. I mean in the evenings. He was on the beach in the morning, too?"

"Every day before breakfast," Jan said. "He'd go for a long walk. Are you saying he was on the beach in the evenings? When? Before dinner?"

"No, late. Quite late. You know I go to bed late - a lifetime of working in the theater where you don't finish work until midnight. I saw him just sitting on the beach. I didn't bother him. Seemed he wanted his privacy."

"That would help explain why he died on the beach, I guess. You might want to mention that to Sheriff Ray."

"Curious. Did you tell the sheriff that Ellersby and I had talked?"

"Thought I'd leave that up to you."

Lolinda smiled. "Thanks. I'll drop into the station later today, although I don't see that it will help much. Enjoy your hike. How's Ms. Lois this morning?"

"She's taking her frustration out on the weeds in the roadside garden."

"I'll be sure to give her a wide berth."

Jan walked with her to the main house and then continued on to her car. Soon she was at the entrance to the park. She smiled as she saw that it was Richard who was on duty at the booth this morning.

The first day she had come here, about two days after her initial arrival in Maine, he had been at the registration booth. She had asked him a ton of questions about the park and where the best locations were to get away from the noise of children. He had asked, with a smile, if she had something against children. She had replied that she was a school teacher on vacation. He had laughed.

Since then they had chatted a few times. She had teased him about being Ranger Rick. He had groaned and replied, "Why do you think I go by Richard?" She had laughed. Today he smiled as he saw her. "Been a few days, Jan. Heard you had some excitement at the B&B."

"Wouldn't exactly call it excitement," she replied.

"No, I can see that. Must be awful having someone commit suicide right at the house."

Jan was relieved to hear that the local rumors were about suicide. "Not exactly at the house but on the beach. Near enough. One of our young guests found him."

"You mean a child? Are they okay?"

"Yeah, he's a well-grounded twelve-year-old. He's coping okay."

"Must help him to have you there. That's the age you teach, isn't it?"

Jan grinned. "You were listening."

He returned the grin. "I always listen. So no vacation even on vacation?"

"It's not bad. Just one kid, and his sister, but they're okay. And today is pure vacation."

"Where are you planning on heading?"

"Any suggestions? I need a vigorous, quiet hike."

"There's the Anvil Trail or the East Trail. They'll both give you a good workout."

"Which do you recommend?"

"Today? I'd take the Anvil Trail. The weather's clear and you should have some nice views at the top of both the Anvil and the Head. Make sure you have lots of water."

Jan hefted her backpack. "Got it all here, Ranger Rick. My whistle and cell phone, too." She grinned.

He pretended to cuff her through the car window. "Get going. Hope you have a good hike. By the way, your suicide liked that trail."

"He was here?"

"Every day. He took the East Trail the first day then stuck to the Anvil. Came with a small daypack - enough for lunch and water and would be out there all day. Didn't strike me as a hiker but you never can tell. First day he didn't leave until 6:00 p.m. The next day was a bit earlier, around 4:30."

"What kind of trail are you sending me on that will take me all day to complete?" she teased.

He laughed. "Should take you an hour and a half or maybe two, depending on how long to enjoy the views."

"Sounds just right," Jan said. "Well, thanks for the advice. Hope you enjoy your day. I should be out well before sunset. In fact, I'll be out before lunch. I only packed a few energy bars."

"See you then," he smiled and waved her through.

She parked, checked her gear and headed for the trailhead. It was early enough to be quite quiet. She knew that it would gradually get a lot busier as the day progressed. Hopefully, she would have a good head start. She just didn't feel like being around people today. As she walked along the well-maintained trail through the woods, she thought about Ellersby coming here. He hadn't looked like a hiker to her either. More like a man at home in an office. Why had he registered under a false name? What did Ted Marston have to hide? And how was it connected to his death?

Chapter 4

Soon enough Jan left the woods behind and started to climb the rocky peaks. She had parked the car at Blueberry Hill and had soon rested briefly on the top of the Anvil, a rocky point rising out of the forest. Then she pushed on to her final destination, the Schoodic Head. She focused on the trail, pushing her stamina to its limits. Soon she was panting too hard to walk any further. She had reached the top and the coast was spread out before her. The Schoodic Peninsula was narrow enough for her to be able to see water on both sides. But she was closer to the eastern side and could see an island out in the bay. She found a large rock to collapse on and pulled out her water bottle. Gradually her breathing and pulse slowed.

The vigorous climb had been just what she needed. She felt her restless energy leave but she still knew that this was just temporary. Another way to escape thinking about her life, or what was left of it. In frustration, she yelled out. It felt good, but then she looked around to see if anyone had heard her. There was no one else on the summit. She shook her head. Yelling at nothing wasn't going to be her solution. Nor was sitting on this rock. She got up and started down the trail.

She hadn't gone too far when she rounded a corner and met a family hiking up. There seemed to be numerous kids jumping and bouncing around. The father greeted her and then said, "Are you all right? We heard some yelling."

"Sorry about that," Jan said. "Just getting rid of some frustration." The parents smiled in understanding. The children just looked at her strangely and then they hiked on past.

Jan thought of those expressions and laughed. Another weird adult, they probably thought. And they were right. She picked up a good pace and was soon enough back at her car. She hadn't thought to bring lunch but was hungry. So she drove around the rest of the park to the exit. The road only went one way in a loop along the coast of the peninsula. Richard was dealing with another hiker so she just waved as she went out.

She went to the cafe that catered to the hiking crowd. She didn't feel like eating in a restaurant and figured she would get a picnic for one and find some quiet place to eat it. She came in out of the sun into the cool dimness of the cafe. There was already a line forming so she took her place. Then she recognized a dark head a few places ahead of her. Lolinda was also there.

After the actress turned with her bag, she saw Jan and came over to talk. "I see we have the same idea. Where are you headed?"

"Don't know yet. Some place quiet that isn't at the B&B."

"You don't want to go back there?"

Jan grinned. "No way. Lois is gardening."

Lolinda smiled and nodded. "And you like gardening as much as you like cooking."

"Exactly!"

"Well, I, too, was looking for a quiet place. Would you mind sharing yours when you find it?"

"Sounds good. I should have my lunch in a few minutes if you can be patient. What did you order?"

"They have this great sandwich of fried mushrooms, sun-dried tomatoes, spinach and cheese on toasted multigrain bread. I'm addicted to it."

"Sounds wonderful. Maybe I'll try the same."

Soon the two women were standing outside the cafe and looking up and down the street. Being summer and the height of tourist season, there were lots of tourists milling around.

"Doesn't look too quiet," Lolinda observed.

"Definitely not. I know it's a bit of a drive but there are some really nice sites in Acadia Park. I have a pass and could probably get you in." Jan was thinking that Richard would let them go in just for lunch.

"That sounds great and don't worry about me. I have a season pass. I get it each year. I like to walk along the trails."

Jan led the way to her car, which was just around the corner. "Shall we go in my car? I can bring you back to retrieve yours later. If it's parked safely."

"It'll be fine. I see you still have your California plates on. So you fit right in with the tourists."

Jan didn't say anything. The car was another thing that she had to figure out since the registration was coming up. Lolinda looked at her. "Sorry, I didn't mean anything by that."

Jan just smiled slightly at her. "Just another thing I have to take care of. The details of life."

"The details make up life."

"What do you mean?" Jan asked.

"I used to think that life was made up of big moments - getting that great role, finding that perfect apartment, meeting that right someone. Then I realized that those moments are just moments. Life is made up of all the rest of the stuff, too. Grocery shopping, finding a parking space, getting your hair done. If you only live during the big moments, you're missing most of life."

Jan thought about that. It seemed to make so much sense. Her life hadn't just been about Greg. It had been about feeding her cat and cleaning the apartment and grading assignments. "You're one very wise lady, Ms. Lolinda."

The actress laughed. "Not so sure about that. I've just lived longer, that's all."

Soon they were back at the gate. Richard was still there. He grinned at her. "Just can't keep away, Jan!"

"This is the only way I get to see you, Richard," she flirted blatantly. He laughed. "And this is my friend, Ms. Lolinda. We're just looking for a quiet place to have a picnic."

"Then I would suggest the Lower Harbor Trail. Not too busy yet. Most people are climbing for higher views today, given the clear skies. And you can come see me any time, Ms. Jan," he grinned back.

They parked near the entrance and started along the trail. Soon they found a picnic table overlooking the water. It was a bit off the trail and seemed secluded by the trees. They unpacked their sandwiches and started eating, both sitting on the same side of the table so they could put their backs to the table top and look out over the view.

"Did you see the sheriff?" Jan asked.

"Yes, I told him about the short conversation but I don't see how it will help any."

"Yeah, but Mr. Ellersby really was playing a role. You were right. How much of what he seemed to be was right? I mean, I thought he was just a businessman. Maybe getting away from the office for a while. It was strange that he came alone. Most people come in pairs or families, especially the men. There seem to be a lot more women who vacation alone." She paused. "That's strange in itself. Why don't men vacation alone? Don't they sometimes just want to get away from it all?"

"Hadn't thought of that myself but you're right. They do seem to travel in pairs or groups. Funny when you think that women are considered to be more naturally social."

"Not me," Jan said. "Lois is the social one."

"You do okay," Lolinda observed.

"It's easy with people like you."

"What do you mean?"

"Well, you don't judge. You don't seem to have any expectations. You're authentic."

Lolinda laughed. "I think that's the nicest compliment anyone has ever given me. Thank you. If I am authentic, it's because I gave up playing roles years ago. And I don't mean in the theater."

"What do you mean?" Jan repeated.

"I just stopped trying to be everyone else's idea of me and focused on being me."

"That would be wonderful," Jan said softly.

"It is but it's not easy. We are surrounded by people who have expectations of us, as you put it."

"Then how did you get there?"

"Probably started when I was young. Being on Broadway was not my parents' idea of a respectable lifestyle. But it was all I wanted. An obsession. Fortunately there were so many of us - I have eight brothers and sisters - they just didn't have the time and energy to fight me. So they let me go. But that wasn't the last role I tried to fit. There were producers and agents, other more successful actors. Everyone telling me what to do, how to be. And I nearly collapsed under the weight. Until I met a brilliant man who showed me who I could be by being myself."

"Did you marry him?"

Lolinda laughed again. "No, he was much older and happily married. He had been a successful actor and was now a teacher. He got me to stop playing other people and to start playing myself. I have never looked back. My career blossomed and my life settled down. I started to enjoy the little things and was always surprised when the big ones came along."

"So you never married?" Jan suddenly stopped. "I'm sorry. I'm prying."

"I don't mind. One thing about being myself is that if I don't like a question I just won't answer it. But that one is fine. No, I never married. I've had friends and good relationships but I'm not looking for permanent."

Jan looked at her and then out at the water. The woman made it seem so simple and clean. Then Jan thought about her own life. It was just a mess. And she truly didn't know who she was. She wanted advice but felt that she had asked enough.

Lolinda waited and then said, "Ask your questions. You're a teacher. You must know that you can never learn if you don't ask. As I said before, if I don't want to answer, I won't. So ask away."

"It's not that. You just make it sound so easy. But life isn't like that. It's messy. Look at Mr. Ellersby. He came here under a false name and then he died on our beach. His death has consequences on young Brad, on my sister, on all of us. He didn't mean to do that. He maybe didn't even mean to die but he did. We may think we control life but we don't. We just go bumbling along and then someone dies on the beach. What can one do about that? We try our best and life jumps up and slaps us hard. So the 'authentic' reaction is to run and hide."

"You're not really asking about Mr. Ellersby, are you?"

Jan stood up and moved towards the water. "Why do you say that?"

"Because we can never know what was authentic for him or why he chose to change his name. I don't mean to pry, but you're talking about yourself. You think your authentic reaction is to run and hide."

Jan sank down to the sand. "It's what I've done all my life. I just leave."

"Leaving isn't the same thing as running," Lolinda said gently. "Are you running?"

"Well, I'm certainly not dealing with it." There was an extended silence and then Jan began to speak. "I thought I had it all figured out. I had run from home because I couldn't be like Lois. I couldn't give them what they wanted - a good housewife, grandchildren. Then I ran from college because they were all so boring and confining. But I stopped when I got to California. I found a job I loved, a place to be me. And then Greg came along. Everyone seemed to think it was perfect. He was good-looking and he said he loved me. But all he wanted was a good housewife and children." She stopped.

"So you broke it off?"

Jan nodded. Then she said the awful part. "On the evening that he proposed to me."

"Oops. It didn't go well, I take it."

"It was brutal and it didn't end there. By the time I got back to school on Monday, he had told everyone how I was a conniving, hard-hearted b…"

"I get the picture. That must have been horrible. When did this happen?"

"Just over three months ago, Jan said with a chest-heaving sigh.

"And Lois said that you've been here two months. What did you do in between?"

"Well, I had to finish out the year. I couldn't just desert my students. So I finished the report cards at the end of the school year and sent them in with my resignation."

"So you didn't run. You left."

"Same thing."

"No," Lolinda said. "It's not the same thing. You fulfilled the obligations that you had to your students, while being in what must have been an awful situation at work. I gather he worked at the same school?"

Jan nodded.

"So you completed the year and then you left. I would have done the same."

"But I abandoned everything - my apartment, my students. At least I hadn't got a new cat since the last one died. So I didn't have to leave that. I knew that Greg didn't like cats so I never got another one, although I would have liked to."

"You didn't abandon them. You finished out the semester. And you should never date a man who doesn't like cats!" Lolinda said with a sparkle in her eyes.

"Is it really that simple?" Jan asked, smiling.

Lolinda nodded and they both started laughing. Jan laughed so hard the tears filled her eyes. She wiped them away and stood up. "Please don't take this the wrong way, but may I hug you?"

Lolinda laughed again and grabbed her in a bear hug. "You're a great person, Jan. If you would just let yourself be."

Jan moved back a bit. "Thanks and I promise to never date a man who doesn't like cats."

"Do you know if Richard likes them?"

"Ms. Lolinda!" Jan said, pretending to be shocked. "We are just friends." Then she grinned. "But I might find out."

"Good. It's important to find these things out early on. Then a lot of suffering can be avoided."

"I think I've learned that. But I still have no clue where I'm going from here."

"So stay awhile until you figure it out."

"If Lois will let me stay. I can't impose on her forever."

"I don't think you're imposing," Lolinda picked up her lunch trash and put it in the covered garbage can. "Do you feel like walking a bit? I gather you've already been hiking today?"

"I went up to Schoodic Head this morning but I don't mind walking some more. I would like to give Lois some more time to finish those flowerbeds." She chuckled. They walked easily along the trail. Then Jan said, "You are one of nine children? That must have been chaos!"

"I'm sure it was, particularly for my mother. But it was good. I'm a middle child so I was left pretty much to myself. My siblings would sometimes agree to act in my 'plays' and my elder sister was a whiz at making costumes from nothing. But all just went along fighting and helping each other. Most have stayed in New York but some have moved away. My mom has lots of grandchildren and even great-grandchildren, so she's happy."

"She's still alive?"

"A feisty ninety-three. Still laying down the law and wondering when I will meet 'someone nice' and get a 'real job.'" Lolinda used her hands for the quotation marks. Then she laughed. "But she definitely is authentic. You always know just what she thinks. No doubt at all."

"I don't know who my mother really was," Jan admitted. "We never seemed to have been able to understand each other. She passed away two years ago."

"I met her when I first came here. She seemed like a nice person. Quiet and nice. I can see her in some of your expressions."

"Really? I think Lois is much more like her."

"In personality maybe. But Lois is real enough. She does a great job running that B&B. I've been coming to this coast for nearly fifteen years. Hers is the first place that I've wanted to return to. She has such wonderful breakfasts and she never intrudes. Having a room in the separate guest house is a bonus."

"Even with the current housemate?" Jan joked.

"Even with her," Lolinda laughed. "Actually last year I had the place to myself. It's a bit lonely that way, even though we have our separate rooms. So I like having a housemate. But back to your sister, she's making a go of this and I think it suits her perfectly. She's almost always fully booked."

"I hope it stays that way. She does seem to be content. But she's worried about the effect of Mr. Ellersby's death. That rumors will hurt her business. Although I heard only this morning that everyone is looking at it as a suicide."

"And maybe it was. Have they found any of his family?"

"I don't know," Jan admitted. "Maybe they can now that they know his real name."

Lolinda stopped. "Maybe we could turn around here. I still have to plan my dinner and I have a friend I'm supposed to call this evening."

"I should be getting back. See if Lois has any jobs for me to do. Hopefully the garden will be finished by now."

They headed back on the trail. Jan said, "You said that Lois was happy. I think she's always been herself. She and John were perfect together."

"John was her husband who died?" Lolinda asked.

"Yes, it was just off the coast here. He was out deep sea fishing. The whole boat was lost. That was four years ago."

"When she bought the B&B?"

"Yeah, she bought it with our mother. Maine has always been a special place for our family. I guess it was the one place that was different. We came here once as little girls. It seems to have held its spell on us since then. Definitely for Lois. She and her husband used to come here every year, once they could afford it."

"Where did they live the rest of the year?"

"In New York City," Jan smiled. "Probably not the same New York City as you live in."

"Probably not. I know they have a son," Lolinda said. "I met him the first year I came. This is the first time he hasn't been here."

"He's at college somewhere."

They walked for a bit longer. This time it was Lolinda who broke the silence. "If you are interested in family relationships, you might want to strike up a conversation with Frau Traeger. She has some interesting ideas."

"What do you mean?"

"I won't give you any details but we had an intriguing conversation that day that we went shopping together. You know that they don't have any children, don't you?"

"I think I heard that. Why not?"

Lolinda smiled. "I'll leave that to you to find out. Since you're investigating family expectations. Everyone is different, no matter how much we are alike. You never know when Mr. Right will show up."

"What? You, too? You sound just like Lois. And my mother!"

Lolinda laughed. "I didn't mean to. I'm just saying we never know what's around the corner."

"And for you, Ms. Lolinda?" Jan asked innocently.

"You're a naughty one, Ms. Jan Cathcart. Just for your information, I have a very nice gentleman right now. And he's not even in the acting business, which makes a refreshing change."

"Is he your phone call this evening? Why isn't he here?" Jan teased.

"Saucy, too. He happens to be at a conference in Las Vegas. Talk about role playing. Las Vegas is all fake. Fascinating the first time. Nauseating after that. No authenticity at all. And, he doesn't want me to change my ways for him. He know how I value this annual getaway."

"You're lucky."

"Just keep your eyes open and be yourself. And remember that it's perfectly okay to be perfectly okay alone. Being alone and being lonely are two very different things."

"As I said before, Ms. Lolinda, you are one wise lady."

Lolinda bowed and they continued walking. Shortly, they were at the parking lot. Jan drove Lolinda to her car. Then she returned to the B&B. She was worried to see the police car once again parked in the driveway. She hurried around to the door on the beach and went in. Lois and Ray were sitting at one of the tables. The constable was back at his place by the door, notebook in hand.

"What's going on?" Jan asked abruptly. Lois looked pale and had her hand on her face.

"Sit down, Jan," Ray said. "I got some news that I thought you both should know. I heard back from the search for Ted Marston, you know, his real name. There's a warrant for his arrest in Missouri."

"His arrest? For what?"

"Embezzlement. He and his partner embezzled their company for nearly a million dollars. His partner has been arrested but Marston ran. Well, now we've found him, dead on your beach and we've got some of the money."

"What do you mean - some of the money?"

"He withdrew over $500,000 on his trip across the country. Lots in cash and more in traveler's checks. That's what was in that suitcase. At least $230,000 was there. The police in Missouri want to know where the rest of the money is."

"He thinks someone here took it," Lois said.

Ray objected, "Wait a minute. I didn't say that!"

"You didn't have to," Lois replied heavily. "You're here. It's obviously what you think. So we not only had an embezzler staying here but also a thief."

"Is that true?" Jan asked.

"That's jumping to conclusions. Maybe he put it in a safe place during his journey. Maybe he stashed it in a bank under his new name. We're still investigating."

Jan looked out the window for a moment. "If he had nearly half a million dollars with him, why would he kill himself? It doesn't make sense."

"No, it doesn't," Sheriff Ray agreed slowly.

Jan felt her chest constrict. Her voice was very quiet. "So we may have a murderer here, too."

Chapter 5

After issuing a warning about keeping it all quiet, Sheriff Ray left. Jan sat down beside Lois. She drank her coffee slowly, giving her sister some time. Finally Lois looked up. "What am I going to do, Jan?"

"You're going to do what you always do. You're going to keep looking after your guests and making breakfasts and, with my help, keep the place going. Leave the rest up to the police."

"But...a suicide was bad enough. But murder?"

"The rumor in town is suicide. It should stay that way. And people weren't blaming you. They were saying what a shame it was that it had happened and they felt sorry for you, wanted to help you. You'll be okay and so will The Elusive Cat. Lolinda said that this is the only place she's found here, after fifteen years of visits, that she likes to stay at. You have something good here, Lois. You've built it up and you can depend on it."

"But it will get out," Lois protested.

"Why? How? Only the police and we know. And you heard Sheriff Ray. He told us not to speak about this and I'm sure he told his constables the same thing. Actually, in one way this is probably a good thing. Chances are he was killed because of that money and it has nothing to do with you or your guests." She put her hand on her arm and stood up. "Come on. You promised me dinner."

Lois looked at her in confusion for a moment and then said, "Oh, yeah. Right. I was going to try a new recipe for shepherd's pie."

"So first we find a shepherd," Jan said in a singsong voice. They both laughed. It had been one of their dad's standard jokes.

Lois started calling out the list of ingredients and Jan fetched them. Soon Jan was chopping and Lois was mixing. She looked up from her bowl and looked at her younger sister. "Thanks, Jan."

"No problem," Jan replied easily. "What sisters are for? And besides, I'm getting hungry. I walked a lot today."

"Where did you go?"

"First, I climbed the Anvil and Schoodic Head. Then I ran into Lolinda at that lunch place and we walked the Lower Harbor Trail."

"She's a nice lady, isn't she?"

"She's amazing! She was telling me about her life. She's one of nine children! Can you imagine? That's like living in one of my classrooms every day and night."

Lois laughed. "Probably not that bad. They would have been all ages and the older would have helped with the younger. But it would definitely be busy."

"Didn't you and John want more kids after John Jr.?" Jan asked.

"Not really. I mean, Johnnie is wonderful and I wouldn't change a thing but kids are hard work. John was really moving up in his career. And I had lots to do to keep up with that. We decided that one was enough. What about you? Don't you want to have your own some day? I mean, you love kids."

"I love preteens and that's the problem. I just about have a panic attack if I think I might have to teach a kindergarten class. And then I hear some of the older teens talking and they sound so arrogant and hard. I don't think I'd be a good mom except for those few years between child and teenager. And, as you say, parenting is hard work. I see and talk with the parents of my students and I don't think I want the worry. My life is just great." Her voice dropped. "Or at least it used to be."

"What happened, Jan?"

Jan looked down at the potatoes she was cubing. She owed her sister something. This was the first time they had ever talked like this, about the important things in life. She had to say something. She took a deep breath. "There was a guy and things went wrong. He didn't take it well. He worked at the same school and he made it impossible for me to stay there. I had to leave."

"What do you mean you had to leave?" Lois looked perplexed or possibly disappointed. Jan couldn't tell the difference sometimes.

"It was just not good. For the students, for me. I had to go."

"So you left your job? What are you going to do now?"

"I don't know. I'll be moving along soon. I really appreciate you taking me in but I know that I'm costing you money by staying here. You could have a paying guest in my room."

Lois looked up from the frying pan on the stove where she was cooking onions. "Actually, you're saving me money. I had decided that it was just too much work to do this all by myself. I used to have quiet weeks when I could catch up but now I'm booked solidly from May through October. And I'm getting more bookings for the off-season, too. I was looking around for someone to help out. So if you want to stay, I could use the help."

Jan put down her knife and looked at her sister. "Do you mean it? This isn't just big sister taking care of hopeless younger sister?"

"I'm serious, Jan. I can even show you the classified ad I was writing to put in the local paper for help. And you're not hopeless. You just need a break. I get that. And you are a big help here."

"Washing pots and chasing spiderwebs," Jan smiled.

"That but also dealing with the guests. Before you came, they were always wandering into the kitchen to ask me questions about sites and places. Now they ask you and stay out of here, which I really like."

"But I can't answer most of their questions. I've only been here a couple of months."

"Last week, I heard you recommending some restaurants to a guest. You've learned more than you know. This isn't a big place. You're learning your way around and the guests like talking with you. I've noticed. And look at the Tipton kids. They practically want to adopt you."

Jan grinned. "They're good kids and they're the right age. Okay, if you want me to stick around to wash pots, I really would like to stay. You have a nice place here. I see why you like it. I'll even help with the garden," she groaned dramatically.

Lois laughed again. "I wouldn't force that on you. Besides, I quite enjoy it."

"Very weird. Anyways, here are the potatoes. What's next, boss?"

"Carrots."

"Aye, aye." Jan threw a sloppy salute and the sisters continued to work together. Jan went into the fridge to get the carrots. "What's this paper bag in the fridge which says in large letters 'Don't touch'?"

"That's Frau Traeger's medicine. She takes it once a week and it has to be kept in the fridge. I believe it's an injection."

"She gives herself a needle each week?" Jan cringed. "What is it? Diabetes?"

"I think she mentioned it was arthritis, some sort of new drug. Just leave it there and get working on those carrots."

"Yes, sir."

Lois shot her a look.

Once the casserole was in the oven, they sat at the kitchen table.

"But seriously, Jan," Lois asked. "What should I do? Ray seems to think that I was careless or even criminal when I didn't check his ID. But I respect people's privacy. As long as they pay for the room and don't cause problems, their lives are their own. I admit it was a bit strange. He booked at the last minute. He came alone and I don't think I've ever had a single man that young come here alone. I did have an elderly gentleman once. He also paid with traveler's checks when almost everyone these days uses credit cards. But the checks were good and he was polite. How was I to guess that he was an embezzler?"

"You couldn't have. I think Ray is a bit out of his depths on this one. He's probably never handled a case like this. If he's ever had a murder before, it was probably domestic violence and they caught the killer at the scene. And we still can't rule out suicide. Maybe Matthew, or Ted, or whoever he was, felt remorse about what he had done."

"Would have been nice if he'd left a note to that effect," Lois commented.

"Yes, it would. Did Ray mention what kind of poison it was? He looked so peaceful lying on the beach. Almost as if he had fallen asleep. According to TV, most poisons are more violent than that."

"Ray hasn't told me anything. And I don't like to think about it. Let's talk about something else."

Jan realized that Lois couldn't see this in any light but as a disaster for herself. Jan was starting to think of it more as a puzzle but she would have to examine it by herself. She searched around for another topic. "Lolinda mentioned that John Jr. was here every other year when she came but he's not here now. Where is he?"

"He had a chance at a work co-op. He felt bad about not coming here to help for the summer but I told him he had to take it. So often those summer jobs lead to full-time jobs after graduation."

"How long until he graduates?"

"He just finished his second year. So two more years."

"I haven't seen him for years. Too bad I'll miss him."

"Maybe you won't. He has a week off between the end of the co-op and the start of classes. He'll be here the beginning of September, which is in about three weeks."

"It's that soon until September?" Jan asked shocked.

"Yes, why?"

Jan shook her head. "Nothing, it's just that this will be the first year I haven't been madly preparing for the start of school. It's strange, that's all."

"Are you going back to teaching?" Lois asked.

Jan stood up. "At this point, I'm going for a quick swim before that casserole comes out of the oven. Join me?"

"You go ahead. I have some work to do."

As Jan swam leisurely out to the buoy, she remembered that she hadn't watched the tide levels yet. She knew that high tide was usually sometime before lunch so it would be low tide now. Not that it mattered. The sheriff said that Ellersby hadn't drowned. She should probably start thinking of him as Marston but Ellersby was how she'd known him. Actually, the tide might matter if he was below the high-water mark. If he had died after the tide had gone out, he wouldn't have been wet. That would move his death to well before midnight. What was he doing on the beach at that time? He hadn't been dressed for swimming. And how had he been poisoned? What kind of poison gave a peaceful death?

She swam back to the shore at a faster pace. She had some research to do on the internet. Why was she bothering? She rationalized that if she could at least prove that it wasn't anyone at The Elusive Cat then that would help Lois. But, to be honest, she loved puzzles. She was thinking of buying some jigsaw puzzles for the B&B so that people could do them on rainy days. But she loved any kind of puzzle. And the questions surrounding Ellersby's death were a puzzle. It wouldn't hurt and it was certainly keeping her mind off the past. And, she admitted, that was the real reason. Any distraction was welcome.

She booted up her laptop in her room. She hadn't used it much since getting here. She didn't want to see what was on social media and she didn't need to hear from anyone in California right now. So she would just boot up the search engine and stay away from the personal stuff. A quick search on high tides said that it was around 11:00 p.m. She would try to be out there tonight to see how high it came. The tides in this area were rather dramatic and significantly changed the beach area.

Then she delved into a study on poisons. She briefly laughed when she thought about the marketing Artificial

Intelligence program trying to figure out her likes and dislikes. She hoped she didn't get inundated with links to drug addiction sites after this! She ran through the opioids, including morphine, but the death was usually violent. Then she looked up what they used to euthanize people in countries where doctor-assisted death was legal. That would be a gentle death certainly. The answer was barbiturates but they needed to be injected. Didn't that make it more likely to be suicide? He wouldn't have sat still for a murder by injection. There would have been some signs of a struggle. Unless he didn't die on the beach but was moved there later.

There were just too many unknowns, Jan decided. Maybe she could work on the motive instead of the means. The 'why,' not the 'how'. One curious point was that only half the money was missing. If Ellersby stashed it somewhere, why didn't he stash most of it? He wouldn't need nearly a quarter of a million for any travel plans. And, if it were stolen, then why not all? Half was a strange amount either way.

Glancing at the clock, she realized that dinner was probably ready. She could work on this later. Make a list of the questions and ways to find the answers. She shut everything down and went to have a quiet dinner with Lois.

By about 8:00 that evening, nearly everyone was in the family room. The two kids were playing a board game with Jan and Lois. It was *Monopoly* and Jan was losing terribly. She was nearly bankrupt. She landed on one of Josie's properties and couldn't pay the rent. So she declared bankruptcy and handed all her property to Josie. "And this, folks, is why it is my sister that owns the B&B," she declared as she got up from the table. Everyone laughed.

She got herself a cup of hot tea and joined the adults scattered around the couches and chairs in the center of the room. They had been discussing plans for the next day. "So what has been decided?" she asked.

Judy smiled. "Nothing. Scott wants to hike but I don't."

"What would you like to do?"

"Well, there is this historical tour of the town and area tomorrow which I thought might be interesting."

Lois spoke up from the games table, "Jan, you should go on that. It is really very interesting. You'd enjoy it."

"I suppose that would be okay," Scott Tipton said reluctantly.

Jan smiled and turned to the Traegers. "And have you made plans?"

Herr Traeger said, "I like the idea of a hike in the national park. Didn't you go there today, Jan?"

"Yes, I took the Anvil Trail which leads you up both the Anvil and the Schoodic Head. Beautiful views from up there. And not too vigorous a hike." She looked at Frau Traeger, wondering if she would be able to do the hike.

Frau Traeger saw her look and said, "That history tour sounds fascinating. I'd really rather do that."

"Sounds like we have a gender divide," Jan teased. "Might I suggest that we women do the tour and let the men do their hike?"

They all exchanged glances with their spouses and then nodded in agreement. Then Scott said, "You women just want to learn more about the pirates and their secret stashes."

Jan laughed but she couldn't help thinking about Mr. Ellersby's hidden treasure. There was a loud groan from the game table as Lois landed on Brad's Broadway hotel. Frau Traeger got up from the couch to go watch the game. Jan turned in her chair and faced Herr Traeger. "Do you hike a lot in Germany?" she asked.

"I used to hike all the time. We have beautiful mountains in Germany. Poor Mr. Ellersby wanted to visit my country and see the mountains. He told me that he really liked to hike."

"Yes, I heard that he went to the National Park a lot. You should enjoy climbing the Schoodic Head. It goes above the treeline and you get a great view of the ocean. Where do you live in Germany?"

"We're near the Harz Mountains in the city of Kassel. My family has lived there for many generations. But we also have a branch on my mother's side which came to the United States in 1712. They landed in New York and then settled in Pennsylvania. I have been checking on the computer for the genealogy but their name, Wanamaker, is very common. I'm hoping to be able to check some documents in New York City to see if I can find when they landed."

"That's fascinating," Jan said. "I've never thought about researching our history. For as far back as I know, we've always lived in Missouri but we must have come from somewhere."

"Your sister told me your last name when we were introduced but I'm sorry I've forgotten it."

"Cathcart. Sounds British maybe."

"You can check. They have wonderful sites on the computers now which let you look at documents and records."

"And what about Frau Traeger? Is she also from the same area of Germany?"

Herr Traeger shook his head. "She's from the south near Freiberg. She didn't have much knowledge of her family. But she has helped me to find mine. She was the one who heard about these lists they kept as the immigrants came into New York."

There was a cheer from the game table. Brad was standing up with his hands in a victory clasp. Lois was grinning. Josie said, "The slum landlord wins again. Don't know how you do it."

"Just brains, I guess," Brad replied, teasing.

"And a good dose of toughness," Lois added. "You are a hard negotiator. Maybe you should be a lawyer."

They put the game away and then the kids wanted to go for a night swim. Judy agreed to go out and watch them. Lois excused herself, saying that she had some paperwork to catch up on. Herr Traeger went over to

Scott to discuss the hike the next day. Jan saw Frau Traeger sitting alone so decided to keep her company.

She tossed around in her head an opening question to start the conversation. Then she thought of the proposed tour. "Do you like history?"

The older woman smiled. "I think we can learn a lot about people from their history."

"Your husband was telling me that some members of his family came to the United States in the early 1700s. I didn't realize one could go that far back in the records."

"Oh, yes. There are lots of records - births, deaths, marriages, even some tax records. It's like a game, a puzzle to figure it out."

Jan laughed. "Well, I love puzzles so maybe I'll try it."

"I did a bit of research on my mother's family. Her name was Turcotte. I learned the name came from France but I didn't have enough details. I knew nothing about my grandparents and my mother died quite young. You need to have some names and some dates to get started. Also, much was destroyed during the war. I have enjoyed researching Rolf's family. They have been quite notable over the generations. There was even a town mayor and a general in the military."

115

"Well, that's fascinating. It must have been hard to lose your mother young. Our mother passed away two years ago. She was only sixty-one. It was cancer."

"The same with my mother but she was only forty-three. Cancer of the liver. And my brother died of the same when he was just thirty-two. A terrible, terrible way to die. I wouldn't want to die like that. I was eighteen when she passed and twenty-eight when I lost Hans. I had just married Rolf and that is why we decided to not have children. The chance of passing the gene along would be too great. But my brother had a little girl, my niece. She has been like a daughter to me. She lives in Missouri but she couldn't see us this visit. She is very busy raising two children and working in a lawyer's office. We practically raised her as our own, taking her on summer holidays when her mother had to work."

"That's wonderful. You know that Lois and I grew up in Missouri."

"A small world, as they say," the older woman said.

"Indeed," Jan agreed, "Lois' son, John Jr., is my nephew. He's usually here in the summer but she said that he got a job through his college this year so he stayed there. I'm hoping to see him when he visits between semesters."

"You have no children of your own?"

"No. I get quite enough of children in my classroom. I'm a teacher usually in California. Just staying here for a while to help Lois."

"She must love having you here. I could have wished for a sister."

"Hilde," Herr Traeger called. "We really should be getting our rest for our busy day tomorrow."

"Of course, mein lieber. Coming right now. It was pleasant talking with you, Ms. Jan. I look forward to our tour tomorrow."

"Good night, Frau Traeger."

Scott went out to check on his family and Jan tidied up the coffee cups and glasses. She turned out the lights in the family room, leaving one on in the breakfast room for the returning swimmers. She popped her head in her sister's room and said good night. Then she went back to the guest house. Lolinda was already in her room, as Jan could hear soft music coming from there.

Jan felt too restless to go to bed just yet. Then she remembered that she had planned to stay up until the high tide which, according to the computer, was at 11:07 tonight. So she sat on her bed and turned on the laptop. She discovered that Cathcart was a Scottish name derived from people who lived in the Cathcart part of Scotland near Glasgow. They were named after the Cart River. She found it on a map. She had never known that there was a Scottish connection. How could she find out when they came over to the States? She got buried in the searches.

It was nearly 11:30 when she next looked at the time. She left the computer on the bed and put on a sweater. She took a flashlight with her so that she could see the high-water mark. She had read that it took just over six hours for the tides to change so it should be still near its highest reach, even though she had missed the high tide point. She quietly went out, although she saw that her housemate's light was still on. As she walked down the path towards the beach, she saw a familiar little gray shape. The kitten was just sitting there watching the water. Jan approached him, but not closely enough to scare him away. "You really are a night creature. But it's nice to have the company. Let me just check the water level."

She went over to where she could make out the police tape in the light of her flashlight. The water covered the entire area. The sand around the cordoned-off square was smooth and wiped clear of footprints. "So he could have died when the water was lower and then been soaked as it came in. Which means he would have had to have died before 10:00 p.m. at least, if not earlier. Why didn't Lolinda see him when she came in? I think she was late that evening." The kitten just stared at her. Jan sat down where the sand was still dry and warm. "Let me remember. That would have been Tuesday night. What did I do that day?"

The cat looked back at the water. "You're no help. Let's see. Of course, that was the afternoon of the petit fours. How could I ever forget that? So Lois was in the kitchen all afternoon and I was answering the phone and washing all the sheets that we had changed on the weekend for the new guests. No clue what the Tiptons had done but they changed for dinner, came back, played cards, I think in the back room while enjoying the treats. Then they went up to bed. About the same time as the Traegers. Would have been about 9:00 or so."

She stared a moment at the waves. Then she snapped her fingers. The cat just glanced at her. "That's right. It was early. I was surprised but I guess they were tired. I remember checking the kitchen and seeing the covered plate with Mr. Ellersby's name on it. Then I left. I didn't see anyone on the beach," she told the kitten. "So he wasn't there at 9:00. And Lolinda wasn't in her room, either. But she was there the next morning. So she must have come in late. Maybe she saw something. How could she have missed him? But why didn't she say anything?" She looked at her companion, who was again watching her. "You know, you're not really contributing much. You probably saw the whole thing. Wish you could speak. It must have happened in that short space of time between 9:00 and high tide at 11:00. I mean, he wouldn't sit down in the water in his clothes. That part of the beach had to be dry when he sat there. Near the edge but still dry. Unless he didn't die here and was placed here."

She shook her head. "No, that doesn't work. Because he would have had to be put here before the high tide. Although he could have been dumped closer to 11:00, which gives us more time. But then there should have been footprints in the freshly wet sand."

To check this, she walked down to the receding edge of the bay. Then she shone her light down. Yes, her footprints were clearly marked on the sand. "Wonder if there were marks when Brad found him. We must have messed those up. Need to figure out how to ask him without scaring him. Well, enough questions for tonight, my friend. I, unlike you, don't wear a fur coat and I am getting cold. Thanks for your help," she said sarcastically, smiling.

The little animal turned and walked up the beach to the side of the house and disappeared. Jan shook her head and followed, going up the pathway. This time, Lolinda's light was off. She shut down the computer and went to bed.

The breakfast of French toast and cinnamon raisin oatmeal went smoothly until the sheriff showed up at the end. Jan suspected that he timed it that way deliberately. This time he asked Scott Tipton to go into the back room. His wife looked at him questioningly but he just shrugged his shoulders. Judy smiled at the kids. "Don't worry. The sheriff just has questions. Maybe he thinks Dad might have seen something at some time. Now, back to the discussion, have you decided what you want to do today? Hike or history?"

Brad looked at Josie and then said, "Hike." He turned around in his seat to look at Jan, standing at the counter. "Sorry, Jan. History just sounds too much like school."

She laughed. "That's okay. You'll enjoy the hike. And Josie?"

"The hike for the same reason."

"Okay, then we're all set. Our tour starts at 10:00 but the hike can go whenever. You guys know the place to get a picnic lunch if you want to eat in the park, right?"

Judy answered, "Yes, Jan. They know it. They can go there first. I wonder how long the tour will take."

"Shouldn't go past lunch. Maybe we three women can go someplace. Would that be fine, Frau Traeger?"

"Certainly. That would be nice."

"Okay, ladies. We'll meet here at 9:30 and go in my car."

"Very clear and organized," Judy said.

Lois spoke up from the kitchen. "Years of organizing field trips, right, Jan?"

Everyone laughed. Brad looked out the front window. "Look, there's Cat and Kitty Jr. I'm going to go say good morning."

"They still won't let you pet them," his sister said.

"Can't hurt to keep trying." He left and Josie followed.

Judy nursed her coffee, frequently glancing at the door to the family room. The Traegers went upstairs. Jan started clearing dishes. "What are your plans for today?" she asked Lois.

"Well, the Traegers leave on Sunday at noon and there is a couple arriving Monday morning from Chicago. Fast turnaround for that room. The Tiptons leave next Friday, a week from today. There's a couple arriving Saturday for one room and then two ladies coming in on Sunday. I have to ask Ray when I can use Mr. Ellersby's room again. I have an older couple hoping to come next Wednesday."

"Wow, that's busy. But we can't do much cleaning until they all leave. Just the one room. Why don't you kick your feet up and enjoy the peace and quiet? We will all be gone until the afternoon. It's been quite the week. You deserve it."

"We'll see," was Lois' answer, with a smile. "Wonder what Ray wants with Mr. Tipton."

"I just hope he doesn't keep him too long and ruin our plans for the day."

In fact, it was only twenty minutes more before the two men came out from the back room. Scott signaled his wife and they headed upstairs. The kids came running in from the beach and went up, too.

Ray accepted the coffee from Jan. Lois asked him, "How's it going, Ray?"

"Slowly. Just checking up on some things."

"I was wondering when I can go in and clean that room."

"I'll just take one more look and then we should be done
with it. His car will be towed this afternoon. It's a rental.
He must have left his own car somewhere because the
licence plate was on the warrant."

"Mr. Tipton's not in any kind of trouble, is he?" Jan
asked.

"No, no. Don't worry about it. Just leave this all to me,
ladies. Thank you for the coffee." He headed up the
stairs.

Jan carried his cup into the kitchen, grumbling.

"What's wrong?" Lois asked.

"Oh, nothing. He just irritates me. 'Leave it all to me.'
Like we're helpless little females."

"He's just trying to take care of us," Lois protested.

"I don't need that." She took a deep breath. "Sorry, I
knew a principal at one of the schools where I did my
practicum. He treated the women like that. Like they
couldn't manage on their own. It just bugs me."

124

"You've been alone too long."

"And I intend to stay that way," Jan replied sharply. A sudden image of Greg came into her mind and she left, heading to the beach. A while later, she saw the sheriff leave and drive away. She sat there, thinking about her reaction and Lois'. Lois had always had a man in her life - their father and then John. But she was doing great on her own now. Why couldn't she see that they didn't need men to take care of them? Relationships should be the meeting of equals, not the strong caring for the helpless. It was demeaning.

She saw someone come quickly out of the house. It was Brad. He stopped when he saw her and then came over slowly. He looked upset. "Can I sit here?" he asked.

"Sure, lots of room. What's up?"

"I was in the bathroom and I could hear my parents. The police think that my dad had something to do with that man."

"Why do they think that?"

"Because he stole some money from Dad's company. Dad said the sheriff nearly accused him of killing him and stealing the money. What money? Will my dad go to jail?"

Chapter 6

"Slow down. If they had wanted to arrest him. They would have done so," Jan reassured him. "Back up a moment. Your dad owns a company?"

"No," Brad explained. "I mean where he works. Dad is one of the bosses at the company."

"But that doesn't make sense. You live in California. That man, Ellersby, lived in Missouri."

"Dad's company, you know what I mean, has branches all over. Dad does some traveling to them sometimes."

"Has he ever been to Missouri?"

"I don't think so. New York, quite a bit, and Detroit."

"Then how would he know Mr. Ellersby?"

"Dad said that the sheriff knows about a message that went out about the stealing. It had his picture and all. Dad was upset because he tried to explain that he never looks at work on vacation." Brad looked at Jan. "That's true. I remember a big argument a few years ago because Dad answered his phone when we were at this theme park. Mom threatened to throw his phone away. So he agreed to leave work behind while we're on vacation."

"I'm sure the police will figure that out. They just have a way of making everyone feel guilty. Like the time I got pulled over by the cops and I started worrying about what laws I'd broken. But I had been going the speed limit, or near it."

"So why did he pull you over?"

"Just wanted to tell me that I had a broken brake light. I don't think they can help it. It's the uniform and all. Your dad will be fine. Don't let it spoil your day."

"But what money are they talking about? Was he a thief?"

"Kind of. The police are handling it. I'm sure your dad will be okay."

At that moment Scott called from the door. "Brad! We need to get going. Grab your backpack and hat."

"Coming, Dad." He hopped up. "Thanks." And he ran off.

Jan thought about what she had learned. Ellersby and his partner must have fled with the money over a week ago. If he ditched his car somewhere and got a rental, then he drove across the country. Even considering that he only

128

drove from Missouri, he would have been on the road for a couple of days. The drive was nearly twenty-four hours long. And he arrived here on Sunday afternoon. Scott didn't get here until that evening and he had flown. Supposedly, he had still been in his office on Friday, after the embezzlement had been discovered. Had he seen the picture? Had he recognized the fugitive? Then why hadn't he called the police?

This time it was Judy who called from the door. "Could we go just a few minutes earlier, Jan? I need to get some money before the tour."

"Sure," Jan replied, getting up. "I'll be ready in a minute." She went to her room to change into history tour clothes, comfortable slacks and a light blouse. The other women were ready when she got to the breakfast room.

Jan found the historical tour quite interesting. The town was on what had originally been Wabanaki land. Wabanaki was translated as "Dawnland," which Jan liked. It gave a feeling of a new day. The town itself was established in 1803 as a sort of poor relation of Bar Harbor. The rich elite went to Bar Harbor, the wannabes came to Henry's Harbor.

The really interesting part was the smuggling of alcohol. Nearly seventy years before Prohibition, Maine went legally "dry." But that stopped neither the saloon owners nor the drinkers. Illegal operations continued up to and through Federal Prohibition in 1920. Because of the numerous bays and coves along the shore of Maine, it was easy to smuggle the bootleg whiskey in. They also learned that the term 'bootleg' referred to the habit of drinkers of sliding thin bottles of booze down their high cowboy boots, to hide from the authorities. All in all, it sounded like a wild time in local history. They visited a couple of the saloons that had opened during that time. Then they went by the small local museum to look at artifacts. They were also shown a room in the basement of the museum which had been a "rum room." These rooms were established to house all the confiscated alcohol. Then once a month, the mayor and other city officials would open all the bottles and pour the contents down the drain.

After the tour, the women found a nice restaurant in the middle of town. They ordered lunch and began to talk about the things they had heard.

"It's interesting how people celebrate their criminal pasts," Judy commented. "I mean it was neat to hear about it all but it really was people breaking the law."

"But it was such a silly law," Jan said. "As if all the problems of society would be solved by the elimination of alcohol."

"Drinking does cause problems," Frau Traeger agreed. "But laws are not the way to solve that. People have to be strong and learn to handle it."

"But some people aren't strong," Judy objected. "I'm not saying I'm for prohibition. I like my glass of wine or beer as much as the next person. But not everyone is strong enough to drink responsibly."

"Then we must teach them," the older woman stated.

Jan interceded, "As a teacher, I can say that we should teach about the risks but we also teach about caring for each other. We always tell the kids to use the buddy system if they are going out. To find a friend close enough to tell you when you've had enough."

"But surely not in middle school?" Judy asked, shocked. "That's what you teach, isn't it? They're too young to be drinking. I mean, Brad and Josie don't drink."

"You'd be surprised how many of them do. Often because they see their parents."

"In Germany," Frau Traeger said, "we give them watered-down wine as children. They grow up with it and know how to handle it."

"I think I like that approach better," Jan said. "Then we wouldn't have these huge parties when a kid gets to legal age and is expected to get thoroughly drunk. That's a big problem."

"I guess that's something Scott and I should be discussing soon. Josie is fifteen and, even though the drinking age in California is twenty-one, I know that there is liquor at high school parties. I like your suggestion of having a buddy, Jan."

"That's placing a lot of trust in a friend," Frau Traeger said. "And trust can be difficult."

"That's true and children trust so easily."

"Until they are first betrayed," the older woman said with deep sadness.

Jan wasn't sure what to say. This was obviously a deep pain for the other woman. She could relate because of Greg. Not that he had betrayed her. In fact, according to him, she had been the betrayer. But he had betrayed her image of him. She had thought he was in love with her as a person. It had been shattering to realize that he was in love with the idea of her as his wife and mother of his children. "We all have our moments of betrayal," she said softly.

Judy just nodded. She seemed to be looking inside herself, too. "Trust is fragile but necessary in any relationship."

Jan thought she might be talking about her own marriage. They seemed happy but one never knew. Everyone at the school had assumed she and Greg would get married and therefore she had betrayed their vision, too. "I agree. There must be trust. Whether it is between buddies or with life partners. I can't imagine a marriage without trust."

"But it happens all the time, Jan," the German lady said. "My mother trusted my father but he betrayed us. He left when my brother and I were little. He took everything and left nothing. My mother struggled to keep us fed and it killed her. Now that is something there should be a law against."

"But how would it be worded and enforced?" Judy asked. "Everyone has their own version of the story. Sometimes, like with your father, it seems obvious. But other times. I don't know. No one really knows what goes on behind the bedroom door. A friend of mine recently got divorced and we were all surprised. Turned out he'd been cheating on her for over a year. I don't see how she didn't know. How could he have done that and she didn't know?"

"Because she trusted him," Frau Traeger stated. "And when you trust, you do not question."

Jan realized that was what had happened to her. She had never questioned because she had trusted her idea of him. She had trusted that version. "That's true," she said. "When you trust, you don't even see the signs."

"My niece, you remember I told you about her, Jan? She was the same. We could see that he was not good but she loved him. And then she finally opened her eyes and she had to leave. For the sake of the children. He gave them a little and then went on to live his life of luxury while they struggled. That is betrayal."

"All I can say is that relationships are complicated," Judy said.

Jan gave a slight laugh. "That's because people are complicated. Can we ever truly know another? I'm beginning to doubt it. But Frau Traeger, you and your husband have been married for many years."

"Forty years next May," she said with pride.

"That's wonderful. So you must have a good degree of trust."

"Of course. With our hopes and fears. But we keep separate bank accounts. That way we each will be okay if anything happens."

"Separate accounts?" Judy asked. "Doesn't he mind that?"

"No. We have always had it this way. We keep half of our money in each one."

"We share all our accounts. I don't think Scott would like me having my own account. Not that we'd have much to put into it. Teenagers are expensive." She gave a twisted smile.

"You should reconsider that, Judy," Jan said. "If something were to happen to Scott, all the accounts could be frozen until after probate. That can take some time. Lois and I went through this with our mother when Dad died. The banks would only give her living expenses until the will had cleared probate. It took nearly eight months to clear. The lawyer told us that our mother should have had at least one account in her own name."

"I didn't know that," Judy said. "I mean we have wills because of the kids but I guess I just assumed that it would all transfer immediately to me."

"It varies by state, but you should look into it. But, on a more serious topic, ladies, I'd like to know what effect all that liquor poured down the drains had on the water supply. Were there a whole lot of drunk fish the day after?"

They all laughed. "What if it went back into the town water?" Judy suggested.

"A big party the following day," Jan said. At that moment, their ordered lunches appeared and they started eating. After a bit, Jan said, "I'm finding this history stuff fascinating. History for middle school is not really in-depth. We do Christopher Columbus and the natives and settlers. Not much about bootleggers."

"Maybe you should suggest a change in the curriculum?" Judy said, smiling.

"Not sure the powers that be would like the kids to learn about that part of their ancestry."

"Why not? It's all part of it. I've always heard rumors that my family descends from gold diggers from the '49 Gold Rush."

"Frau Traeger's husband was telling me about researching his family's history. He even found a link to

New York City. I did a bit of searching last night and found that my name comes from Scotland."

"So you're more a whiskey girl than a rum girl?" Judy laughed.

"Actually, I prefer vodka," Jan grinned. "Maybe there's a secret Russian connection."

Their plates were cleared and they all ordered hot tea. No one seemed eager to leave yet. They chatted a bit about family stories. They were each from a different generation and place and yet many of the stories had a common theme. Some bragging about illustrious ancestors and some silly stories. Judy shared one about her great-great-great-grandfather being sent out to the front steps to watch the bread rise when his wife was displeased with him. Frau Traeger said that her husband told a similar one about his great-grandfather having to hide out with the horses in the stables when his wife was on a rampage.

Jan laughed a fair bit. "Women sure knew how to treat their men in those days!"

"As long as we control the kitchen and the food, we are in charge," Frau Traeger said, smiling.

"Lois would agree with you there. Guess I should stay single until I learn to cook." She looked at her watch. "Speaking of Lois, I should probably be heading back to help her. Is there anything else you ladies want to do in town before we go?"

"I'm fine," Judy said. "What I would like is a quiet swim before the men get back and Brad decides to splash everyone."

"I admit that I could use a rest myself," the older woman said.

"Then let's head home. I have really enjoyed myself. Thanks, Judy, for suggesting this."

"And thank you, Jan, for sending the men on their way."

They arrived home to find the men and kids already in the water. "So much for your quiet swim," Jan said.

"That's okay," Judy said. "I'm used to it."

Jan couldn't find Lois in the house so she went to her own room. Lolinda was also out. She was restless but couldn't figure out what to do. Her legs were still tired from the tour so a walk along the beach was out. A swim would be nice but not with everyone else there. She would swim later. For distraction, she pulled out her computer. She remembered that she had wanted to make up a list of questions.

She thought about what she had learned so far. Mr. Ellersby had returned after dinner and after everyone else, except Lolinda, had gone to their rooms. He had eaten the petit fours and then, as was his custom, he had gone to the beach. He had died there sometime before 11:00 p.m. She felt it was safe to assume that he had not sat down in the water but above the waves. Lolinda had returned sometime later but had not seen him, despite the fact that the pathway from the parking lot to the guest house went along the edge of the beach.

Then there was the matter of the missing money. Ellersby had spent his days in Acadia Park. He had only taken in a small bag with, she assumed, lunch. So he hadn't buried the money in the park. And it was a silly idea anyways. He wouldn't bury the money. How could he get it later? Which led to - why was he in Maine? Obviously hiding from the authorities but what were his plans? He had spoken to Herr Traeger about Germany. Had he been serious? How could he leave the country under his own passport? Surely there would be notices at the airports for his arrest. People got fake papers all the time in the movies but Jan didn't think it was that simple. And she had no idea how one would go about doing it. Maybe he had realized that this was the end of the road and had killed himself rather than go to jail.

Seemed a bit extreme and where had he gotten the poison? Where was the needle? It could have floated out on the tide but needles were metal so it should have been on the beach. Maybe the police had found it. Then why was Sheriff Ray still coming to ask questions?

Maybe someone from his past life had found him and killed him. Then what about the money? They would have taken it all. They could have found his house and room key on him; searched his room; by some amazing chance, found the secret stash. And taken only half? That made no sense at all. And how would they have found him? The police hadn't been able to, until after he died.

She decided to see what there was about Ted Marston on the internet. There were a lot of references to a Ted Marston who was a professor in Indiana. Finally she found a reference in an obituary notice from five years ago for a Regina Turcotte of Warrensburg, Missouri. Survived by her three children Douglas (Jane), Jennifer Marston (Ted), and Bonnie Craig (Dave). So he had a wife. Some grandchildren were also listed but not which couples they came from. So there could be some children who had lost their dad. Hopefully, the police had contacted them.

There were no other references, which made sense if he were working as an embezzler. He would want to stay private. Out of curiosity, Jan checked her own name.

Outside of her social accounts, which she ignored, she was listed in both the obituaries for her parents and that of Lois' husband, John. That was the extent of her presence on the cybernet. She looked for a moment to the social media listings but still didn't want to touch that. It connected too closely to the life that she had left. She shut the laptop and checked the beach. No swimmers. Perfect.

The Tiptons had decided to order in dinner that evening. Everyone was too tired to go out. They invited Jan and Lois to join them. Lois contributed a cake that she made and Jan fetched the dishes and silverware, adding a bottle of wine which she had bought to share with Lois.

They had a wonderful dinner of fried chicken and all the fixings. The conversation revolved around the day's adventures of hiking and history. After dinner, the kids suggested a card game. Lois and Jan got up to clear the table but Judy spoke up, "Lois, sit back down and play the game. You do enough work for all of us. I'll help Jan clean this up."

"Sounds like a plan," Jan said, gently pushing Lois to follow the others into the family room. Jan and Judy stacked plates and carried them into the kitchen. Then Jan started rinsing while Judy loaded the dishwasher. Judy said, "Jan, you should be sitting down, too, but I wanted to talk with you. I think I may have said too much this afternoon - given the wrong impression."

"What do you mean?"

"I was just frustrated but things are good between Scott and me. This has been a really rough year for him. We've been coming to Maine for many years. Previously I would load the kids into our RV, hook up our boat, and drive across the country. It was always an adventure. Then we would find a nice spot to camp and wait for Scott to arrive. He's never been able to get more than two weeks off during August. Once he arrived, we would all move onto the boat and spend two weeks sailing."

She closed the dishwasher and stood looking into the breakfast room. Jan pointed to the little table. "Have a seat. Which would you prefer - coffee or tea?"

"This late, it had better be tea. Thanks." She sat down and waited for Jan to join her after filling the kettle. "This year the boat needed some really serious work done. Perhaps even a new engine. We just couldn't afford it so Scott sold the boat and the RV. That boat was his dream. I think those two weeks on the ocean got him through the rest of the year. But we just couldn't do it. It is getting so expensive to live in the Bay Area. And the kids are getting older. They want to do things that their friends do. It's hard to keep saying we can't. I was set to cancel the whole trip but Scott wouldn't let me do it. He wanted us all to fly but I said it would be better if I came with the kids in the car. We camped along the way. It also gave us a car here. And this place is just what we needed. So beautiful and quiet with the beach right there. You and your sister are amazing. I don't know what you've been saying to Brad but he's the happiest that I've seen him in ages. He's not bottling things inside like he used to."

"I haven't been saying much, just letting him talk. He's a good kid and so is Josie. You and Scott have done a good job, Judy. I'm sorry to hear about your struggles but you seem to be pulling through. That's all we can do at times. I'd forgotten myself how expensive the Bay Area has become until I came here."

"When are you going back?"

"When Lois kicks me out," Jan joked. She got up and made a pot of tea, bringing two cups and the sugar. "Seriously, I have no clue. I kind of like it here."

"Maybe you can find a local teaching job."

"Yes, maybe." They heard some laughter from the back room. "You know there are places that will take you deep sea fishing. You won't find any brochures here because Lois lost her husband on one of those expeditions. It was during a freak storm in the fall. But the weather is good now. There are places in town. I'm sure Scott and the kids would really enjoy that."

"That's a great idea. We'll look into it next week. Thanks. And, by the way, the sheriff this morning was just asking Scott some questions because the dead man worked in one of the branch offices of the company Scott works for."

Jan hesitated a moment and then decided to be honest. "I know. Brad told me."

"How'd he know?!"

"He overheard you talking. He was afraid his dad would be arrested. I just told him that the cops ask questions of everyone."

Judy was thoughtful. "I guess we should discuss it with the kids. They always seem to know more than we think."

"That's kids, for sure."

"Let's just hope the police figure this out soon so we can put it all behind us."

"I think all of us are hoping for that," Jan agreed.

"The sheriff was wasting his time questioning Scott. He didn't know anything. He doesn't bring his work on vacation. So he couldn't help. But it is strange finding out that they worked at the same company. Small world."

"And it gets smaller than that. Turns out Mr. Ellersby was from Missouri, where Lois and I grew up. I don't often meet people from Missouri."

"Too bad you didn't know that before he died. You might have been able to share some memories."

Jan nodded but she doubted he would have admitted to being from there, considering what he did. She remembered her own questions about Scott's knowledge. "I suppose it's hard for Scott not being able to come across the country with the family."

Judy laughed. "Not really. He hates sitting in a car for long. Gets too restless. He's actually quite irritating when we've done shorter trips. The kids and I have our routines. He just disrupts them. And he always takes a few extra days off before he joins us to get work done around the house that he claims he can't do while we're 'in the way'." She put it in air quotes. "I think he just likes to kick back and listen to his music really loudly."

Jan laughed. "I can relate."

Just then the front door opened and the Traegers came in. Jan excused herself to see if they needed anything. Judy went into the back room. The Traegers told Jan that they were tired and would be heading to bed early. Jan decided to head back to her own room. She left her door open, hoping to catch Lolinda when she returned, if it wasn't too late. When she tried to think of something else to research, her mind kept coming back to Tuesday night and the actress' late arrival home. She really liked Lolinda and was worried that it was all a lie. Everywhere she turned, it seemed that people were playing roles. Without Judy's confession, she never would have guessed that they were having financial troubles. She certainly never guessed that Ellersby wasn't who he said he was.

She was used to students playing roles. It's how they figured out who they may want to be. But those roles are blatant and often, silently, amusing. But adults were so much more complicated. Was anyone authentic? Or was everyone just layers and layers of roles imposed by society and our own expectations? Her brain was too tired to think about this and, she suspected, she didn't really want to know the answers. So she opened a solitaire game and played where skill and luck were all that was necessary to win.

She hadn't heard the front door open when Lolinda popped her head in her door. "Working hard?"

Jan smiled. "I think this computer has it in for me. It never gives me the card I need."

"The malevolent machine. And yet you keep playing?"

"Sucker for punishment," Jan laughed, closing the lid.

"What's keeping you up so late?" Lolinda asked.

"Too many thoughts in my brain. Won't let me rest."

"Such as?"

"Don't ask. My brain gets weird sometimes."

"Happens to us all. I just met with an old friend whom I've known for years and he told me about a daughter whom I knew nothing about."

"Roles," Jan mumbled.

"What?"

"That's one of the things I was thinking about. Roles. I know we discussed them before but are we anything but roles? If you take away my roles as daughter, sister, teacher, friend, is there anything left?"

"No wonder you can't sleep. That's a question for a psychologist or a philosopher. What brought this on?"

"I was thinking about Mr. Ellersby. Did you know he was married?"

"Divorced," Lolinda said.

"Really?"

"Well, when he and I were talking about roles, he referred to his ex."

"That might change things."

"In what way?" The actress came further into the room and Jan motioned her to the end of the bed where she sat.

"I was thinking that he might not have committed suicide if he were married. Some thought about responsibility to others. I mean, he seemed a decent sort. But if he were divorced."

"I don't think it was suicide."

"Why not?" Jan asked.

"I was in town late that afternoon, waiting for a friend to pick me up and take me to dinner and I saw him go into the art supply store. Why would someone thinking of ending their life go into an art store?"

"Ellersby was an artist? Never would have thought that."

"Everyone is an artist, Jan."

"Not me. Can't draw a thing. My students laugh when I try."

"That's probably because you were never taught how to draw. As a teacher, you should know that most things have to be learned. We are rarely born knowing how to draw or sing or act. You should take some classes. This is the perfect place. This whole area is teaming with artists."

Jan laughed. "You have no idea what you're asking. I would have to change my name so that it doesn't reflect badly on Lois. I'm that bad."

"Another role? Jan Cathcart - famous artist?" Lolinda was laughing heartily.

After Jan recovered herself, she speculated, "So Mr. Ellersby goes into an art store - for supplies or classes or something. Then he goes for dinner somewhere, comes back here, eats the petit fours and goes to sit on the beach, where he dies. Doesn't make any sense. Did you see anything when you came back that night?"

"Do you know the police asked me the same thing and it's been bothering me. When I got back from dinner with my friend, it was very late. Close to midnight. It was very dark but, as I think you know, I have a mini flashlight in my car. So I started from the parking lot. My flashlight was quite dim but I hoped it would make it here. It didn't. Just as I got near the front of the main house, it died completely. I had to walk so carefully to make sure I stayed on the path around the house. I wasn't looking forward to a midnight swim if I headed the wrong direction." She took a deep breath. "I probably walked right past him or at least on the path above where he was sitting. Maybe I could have done something."

Jan leaned forward and put a hand on the woman's leg. "If you came home at midnight, he was already dead. There was nothing you could have done for him."

"How do you know?"

"Because he was found below the high-tide water mark. High tide is around 11:00. Unless he sat down, fully clothed, in the water, he was there before 11:00."

"Are you sure?"

Jan nodded.

"Well, that makes me feel a bit better. It's still creepy to think that I walked past a corpse but at least there was nothing I could have done to help him." She looked at Jan. "What made you look up the tides?"

"I was curious. I like figuring things out." She gave a crooked smile. "And it keeps my mind off other things."

Lolinda smiled and patted her hand. "Well, hopefully your mind will let you rest some. You have eased my mind and I thank you. Good luck with those cards." She got up and left, saying, "Good night, Jan."

"Good night, Ms. Lolinda."

Jan put away the computer and changed for bed. She was happy that Lolinda was able to explain away the inconsistency. But she had raised new questions. Like that visit to an art store? Why, when he was hiding from the police? And if that ruled out suicide, then who had killed him?

Chapter 7

For breakfast, Lois had prepared a big plate of various fresh muffins beside a large fruit bowl. There was another platter of bacon and she was frying eggs for anyone who wanted them. Jan got there a bit late because she overslept. She was still yawning as she grabbed a banana chocolate chip muffin and headed for the coffee machine. The Tiptons were already down and eating. Judy laughed when she saw Jan. "A late night partying, Jan? Wonder what goes on in that guest house hidden back there."

"You'll never know," Jan quipped back.

When she got into the kitchen, Lois said, "You do look like the morning after."

"Don't worry. We're not throwing wild parties. Just stayed up late chatting with Lolinda. I really like that woman."

"She is a gem. I'm afraid I've really destroyed the kitchen this time." Lois waved her hand at all the bowls and pans on the counters.

"I'm not surprised. These muffins are incredible. When did you start baking?"

Lois smiled. "Some of us work around here, you know."

"Okay, okay. I get the message. Lead me to the sink."
She popped the last bite of muffin in her mouth and
drank some more coffee. Then she started to gather up
the bowls and fill the sink with soapy water.

"No, really, Jan. I didn't mean anything by that. I'm
naturally an early bird. You can finish your breakfast
first."

"I'll just get a bunch done and then I'll be awake enough
to enjoy the food. No problem, Lois. Really." She
scrubbed the first mixing bowl. "So what are the plans
for today?"

"Well, I didn't get Mr. Ellersby's room done yesterday. I
spent the afternoon doing a huge food shopping trip,
hence the fresh fruit salad this morning. So I'll work on
that. What are you up to?"

"I want to head into town sometime but this afternoon is
fine for that. I can help you with the room this morning."

"I would appreciate that. I really want to do a thorough
clean, since we have the time. I mean move all the
furniture to clean under and such. Today's Saturday and
the new guest doesn't arrive until Wednesday. What
were you and Lolinda discussing that late?"

153

Jan laughed. "She was suggesting that I take art classes."

"What? Art classes? But you can't draw. Neither can I. It was one thing we were both terrible at."

"I tried to explain that to her but she said that I shouldn't give up until I'd had a proper teacher. Remember that art teacher in high school? Miss Birch? She hated me."

"Hated me, too. Told me I would never be an artist. The only thing I learned how to do was draw dogwood flowers."

"Dogwood flowers?" Jan said. "Why those?"

"No idea. But they weren't bad. I can still draw them. But nothing else."

"Then I guess you'll just have to take this course with me."

"Are you serious?" Lois asked.

"It would be fun."

"It would be a disaster."

"Probably," Jan admitted. "But I think Lolinda has dared me so I'm going to look into it."

"You're on your own. I have too much to do here." Brad came up to the counter and asked for an egg and Lois went to make it. Jan continued scrubbing the pots. Soon the Traegers came down, and the sisters were both busy, frying eggs and making sure breakfast went smoothly.

The Tiptons had come down early because they were spending the whole day whale watching off the coast. They left just after the Traegers came down. After eggs and coffee, the German couple spread brochures all over their table and began their daily discussion. Jan kept an ear open as she cleared the other dishes. The final choice seemed to be a day spent in Bar Harbor at museums and plans for an indulgent lunch at a renowned seafood restaurant. Jan saw them happily on their way and cleared their table. Then she grabbed a large bowl of fruit and another muffin, apple cinnamon this time.

"Lois, come join me. Everyone is gone and Ms. Lolinda won't be here for another hour or so."

Lois looked around the kitchen and nodded. She got the same breakfast as her sister and a large cup of coffee. She sat down with a sigh. "Nice to get off my feet. I'm glad I only provide breakfast. Some of the inns supply three meals a day."

"You do it all yourself and you prepare such amazing meals. Don't know how you keep coming up with ideas."

"Actually, it's a rather fixed rotation through two weeks. That way few guests get the same meal twice. And then there are variations on themes. Like one week it will be blueberry pancakes and another banana. That sort of thing. It's not that difficult."

"For you," Jan said. "If I were the chef, they'd be eating cold oatmeal and dry toast every day."

Lois laughed. "So we'll leave me as cook, okay?"

"Definitely. I'll stick to washing the pots."

"But that's not right for you, Jan. I mean you're so smart and talented. You can't just be washing pots."

"For now it's fine. And I'm no smarter or more talented than you, Lois."

"Of course you are. Sure I can cook and garden but anyone can do those. You went to college. You're a teacher. You were meant for bigger things."

"You sound like Mom," Jan said.

"She was right. You are better than the rest of us. Meant for more."

Jan pushed her seat back and stood up. "Don't say that! It's not true! I'm a mess. Look at you. You had a husband who loved you. You have a wonderful son who is now at college. You have this great business and everyone admires you. I have nothing. I have wasted my life trying to be someone that Mom dreamed up. I'm no better. I'm a failure."

Lois also stood up. "Don't say that! You're a teacher. There's no better profession. Sure, you hit a rough patch. We all do. But you'll bounce back and go on helping children. I may have one child but you have hundreds."

Jan sat down with tears in her eyes. "That's all gone."

Lois came up behind her and hugged her. "It will come back. You'll see."

Jan shook her head. "I'm not going back to California."

Lois took her own seat. "Okay. Then you can find a school somewhere else."

"It's not that simple. First, I have to find myself. Outside of all these roles that others put on me. Or that I put on myself."

"What are you talking about?" Lois asked.

"Oh, nothing. Just leftovers from late-night musings. Sorry to dump on you. I'll get back to those dishes. The kitchen still needs some help."

"No rush, Jan. You don't have to do this."

Jan stood up and looked her older sister in the eyes. "Yes, I do. I appreciate your help, Lois, but this is something that I have to sort out for myself. Why don't you take a break or check for phone calls while I finish up this kitchen? Then we can tackle that room." She walked back to the sink and filled it again for the next load. She heard her sister get up and leave the room. She chastised herself as she scrubbed. She should have never opened up to Lois. They would never understand each other. To Lois, everything was simple. You played the role you were assigned - wife, mother, cook, caring older sister. Jan needed more. She needed to know if she was anything besides that. She knew that she could never have any authentic relationships or friends until she figured out who she really was. And Lois would never get that. She vowed to keep her insecurities to herself from now on.

Cleaning the room was good hard physical work. And, because the vacuum was running much of the time, there were no more awkward conversations. Lois kept an ear open for Lolinda's arrival and went down to make sure she had everything that she needed. Jan looked around the room. It looked like everything was done. Strange to think that the man who had last slept here was now dead. Well, it happened to everyone.

When Jan thought about death, she usually thought about her mother. She hadn't been here. She hadn't even visited. Lois had carried the burden all by herself. But their mother had probably preferred that. All Jan ever did was irritate her. Jan could remember all the times that her mother would sigh with disappointment - when she brought home less than an "A"; when she refused to take the tutoring job to help younger students at school; when she wouldn't let her help with her prom dress, which was just her regular jean dress with no accessories. Jan had never lived up to her expectations either as a daughter or as a student. And, as an adult, Jan realized that she had done that on purpose. She really would have liked to have made the prom special but she wanted control above all else. If primping for prom meant letting her mom help, then she would go as plain Jan.

Once she had left for college, she never looked back. She knew, from a rare letter from Lois, that their mother had been bitterly disappointed when she had skipped her college graduation. That was to have been her parents' victorious moment - celebrating that they had raised a daughter who now had a college degree. Jan's attitude was that she had done all the work and even paid for it so it was her moment. And if she chose not to share it, that was her prerogative. Now she saw how selfish she had been. She had never been able to break out of the role of rebellious, resentful child. She stood in the empty room and looked over at the guest cottage. That was where the woman who had borne her had died. Since the funeral, Jan had eased her feelings of guilt with the fact that the favorite daughter, the one who had met all expectations, had been there for the end. Now she accepted that she should have come, too. The woman had been her mother. Just that simple. Roles or no roles, that should have been acknowledged. Quietly, she said, "Sorry, Mom."

"What was that?" Lois had come back into the room.

"Oh, nothing. Just gathering cobwebs."

"I thought we cleared all of those."

"Not the ones in my head." Jan saw her sister look at her strangely. "Don't mind me, Lois." She picked up the piled sheets from the bed. "I'll get these down to the laundry room and I guess we're done here."

Lois looked around. "Yes. Thanks for your help. I'll just air out the quilt and leave these windows open for some fresh air."

Jan went down, dropped the sheets in the laundry room, and went into the breakfast room. Lolinda was sitting at one of the small tables in front of the window. "Good morning, Ms. Lolinda."

"Good morning, Jan. Did you finally get some sleep?"

"I slept just fine. I tried to convince Lois to take that art class with me but no go."

"So you're really going to take one?"

"Of course. You dared me and I never refuse a dare. Which, by the way, is the exact opposite of what I teach my students."

Lolinda laughed. "And why is that?"

"Why do I teach them that or why do I not listen to my own advice?"

"The first part. I won't dare to touch the second part."

"I teach impulsive preteens who will accept any dare even if it harms them. I'm sure you've seen some of the stupid stuff that kids put on social media. Crazy dares that have killed some. So I try to teach them to use their brains. To think about the reason for the dare and if the risk is worth the reward. Don't know if it works but I keep trying."

"I think you must be an amazing teacher, Ms. Jan. The kids are lucky to have you."

"I try my best. So what are you up to today?"

"A leisurely day of reading on the beach. I've done enough socializing for now. I still have another week here to see any friends whom I missed."

"Sounds like paradise. I, on the other hand, will be heading into town to make a poor art teacher's life miserable. And it will all be your fault!" They both cracked up. Lois came in, looking at them in question. "Don't worry, big sister. Just your little sis being a pain, as usual."

Lolinda explained, "Jan was telling me that she plans to take an art class. You really should, too, Lois."

"I don't have the time, Ms. Lolinda. And teaching one Cathcart girl art is challenge enough for any teacher." They all laughed.

Jan went back to her room to get her car keys. She had some difficulty finding a parking space since it was the weekend and all the locals had joined the tourists to do their shopping. She finally found one a few blocks off the main street. It was a pleasant walk back towards the center of town. She did some window shopping until she came to the art store, The Art of Being. She pushed through the door and heard the small bell ring. There was an elderly gentleman behind the counter who looked up at her. There were several others browsing around the shelves of papers and canvases and painting/drawing supplies.

"May I help you?" the proprietor asked as she approached.

"I was looking into information about beginner art classes."

"Then you will want to talk with my son. One moment, I'll just get him from the back office."

The son appeared to be in his forties with long brown hair pulled back in a ponytail. He was wearing a white dress shirt and casual dress pants. "I'm Steve. You're interested in classes?"

"Well, yes. I have to warn you that I'm a terrible artist but someone told me that's just because I have never been taught properly. I was hoping you might tell me if there are classes for terrible artists."

The man smiled. "I don't know if I have a class by that name but I do have one for beginners. And your friend is right. Anyone can draw."

"I may prove you wrong. So, when and how much and all those details?"

"Why don't we move to one of the back tables while we discuss what you might need?" He showed her a room behind some curtains at the back. It was actually the whole back half of the store. Obviously this was where the classes took place. There were easels and tables scattered around. He took a seat at one of the tables and motioned her to a chair on the other side.

"Now," he said. "I'll need some details so we can find the best fit. How long will you be in the area? Are you a seasonal visitor?"

"Actually I live at The Elusive Cat B&B."

"A guest?"

"No, the owner's sister."

He nodded. "I heard that a sister had arrived."

"Heard from whom?" Jan asked.

"Just the rumor mill," he smiled. "We don't have much happen here so we chat about new arrivals." Then his face went serious. "Sorry, wasn't thinking. That's the place where that man died. How horrible for you and your sister. People are saying it was suicide."

"It has been hard but the police are looking into it. I think they're trying to trace his movements for the few days he was here. Trying to figure out why."

"I know. They came here and asked questions." Jan just looked at him so he continued. "He dropped in here late that afternoon. The day before he was found on the beach."

"I didn't know that he was an artist," Jan exclaimed.

"I don't think he was. I mean, he didn't buy anything or even look around much. He met a man here."

"He did? I also wasn't aware that he knew anyone here."

"Not sure he did. I shouldn't be talking about this. I mean it is a police investigation, isn't it?"

Jan shrugged. "Not much they can do if he did kill himself. But I think the more that my sister and I know, the easier it will be for us to understand it and put it behind us. She's really worried that it will affect her business."

"I understand that. The only reason I said that I don't think he knew the man is that they didn't shake hands or anything. They talked quite quietly but this is a small shop. I overheard a reference to Germany and some talk about a passport."

"Did you recognize the other man?"

"I've seen him around. Not really an upstanding citizen."

"What do you mean?" Jan asked.

"He's known for getting things for people. Things they can't get legitimately. I wasn't too pleased that he was using my store for a meeting place."

"Known through the rumor mill?" Jan said smiling.

He grinned back. "Yep. Always reliable, except when it isn't. But we haven't talked about your class. If you're going to be here for a few months, I have a weekly class of adult beginners on Wednesday afternoons. Mostly retirees but some others who have flexible work schedules. We work on basic skills and then each person does their own project. I will start you on still life. The best way to start. After some sketching exercises and such."

"You mean 'Apple with Coconut' type thing?"

"Coconuts are hard to come by here, but something like that. Is there anything you would really like to draw?"

Jan hadn't thought much about it. The class was just an excuse to find out about Mr. Ellersby's visit. But now she was intrigued. "Cats," she said impulsively. "I would love to draw cats."

He laughed. "All that glorious fur. That will keep you coming here for years."

"Are they that hard?"

"Not if you're serious. But let's start with shapes, work up to the apples and then we will see. Can I look forward to seeing you next Wednesday? Classes are paid for on a drop-in basis. $25 for an hour and a half."

Jan stood up. "Thank you, Steve. I will try to be here Wednesday. It depends on the state of my courage but I'm intrigued now. Don't know why, but I really think it would be neat to draw cats someday. And, by the way, I'm Jan Cathcart." She held out her hand and they shook.

"Look forward to seeing you, Jan. And if you don't show up, I may come and find you. I know where you live," he teased.

She laughed. "Then I will have to come."

She went out of the store with a smile on her face. Then she thought about what she had learned about Mr. Ellersby. She was starting to put the pieces together and she really should go to the police. Maybe they already had all the information but it couldn't hurt. She pulled out her phone to find the police station and found that it was on the other side of town. Her car was parked between the two places. She would walk. It was such a nice day and she didn't want to take the chance of not being able to find another parking spot.

It took her twenty minutes to get to the station. She went in the entrance and asked to speak with the sheriff. She was asked her name and told to take a seat in the tiny waiting room. The only reading material were pamphlets on crime prevention and the local paper, which she had already read at the B&B. So she stared at the wall and tried to think how she would present her information to Sheriff Ray. Turned out she needn't have bothered. When she was called into his office, he briefly looked up and asked her what she wanted. Then he looked back at the files on his desk.

Jan was irritated but decided to forge ahead. "I just wanted to give you some information about Mr. Ellersby that might help."

"Hard solid evidence?"

"Not exactly…" Jan started.

"Then thank you for coming in but we have concluded the investigation. We've determined that Mr. Ellersby took his own life because he didn't want to go to jail."

"Oh, it's finished?" Jan asked. "Then you found the poison and the needle? And the rest of the money?"

"We are still checking on incoming evidence but it won't change the situation. These are matters for the police, Ms. Cathcart. Please leave them to us. I appreciate you coming in here but it is better if civilians don't meddle. If that is all, I am very busy." He stood up.

Jan felt her anger rising but she had years of learning to suppress it. She stood up herself and left the office before she said something that might not be taken back. But she vented once she was back out on the street. To spare the people around her, she vented silently. Her anger had no words, not yet. She went back to her car and decided that a walk would be best before she went back to the house. She knew that Lois respected Ray Nolan but she found it very hard to do so herself.

As she carefully weaved the car through the crowded narrow streets, she knew that she had to get away from everyone for a while. So she headed for the park. Another ranger was on duty and just waved her through. She parked in the main lot and headed along the beach at a brisk walk. There were others walking but not many. Looking at her watch, she realized that it was past lunch. That should keep the path rather quiet for a bit. Then the words started forming in her head. "Dumb patronizing official! Putting me in my place as a 'civilian.' Didn't even have the decency to listen. Not to some woman. Wonder if being a man might have helped. Probably not. He obviously thinks he's a cut above the rest of us. How can he have decided it was suicide? And he said they were still gathering evidence. You don't make a verdict without all the evidence." Well, she had done her civic duty. She had tried to tell him the factors that made suicide unlikely. Not her fault if he didn't want to listen. She would just have to figure out a different way.

She kept walking as the words spun around and around. Every time she thought about the way he had dismissed her, she flared again. Then slowly she started to put him aside. He was who he was. In a small town like this, the sheriff was seen as an important person. Lois saw him that way. Jan was more independent in her judgment of people. They had to earn her respect by the way they acted, not just by their title.

She had met too many people in education who thought that they should be listened to just because they had a position, like director of education or school board trustee. Many of them knew little or nothing about teaching. They just knew how to run a business and please those paying the bills. For years, she had ranted that the children got lost in the shuffle. It was one of the reasons that she had chosen to work in the private system. But it still happened there. People were admired for how much funding they brought, not how happy their students were. And teachers were praised when their students got high scores on the national tests but not when their students learned to stand up for themselves or defended a friend.

Maybe organized education wasn't really the place for her. She wanted to work with children where she could celebrate their growth as complete human beings. Maybe it had been time for her to leave the school, even if she had been forced out by Greg. Maybe he had actually done her a favor. It was a curious thought and one that excited her. Instead of a ruin of a past, she started to see the next horizon. Her pace slowed and she realized that she should turn back. She hadn't eaten anything since breakfast and, at this rate, she might also miss dinner. Lois had mentioned that she would cook for both of them as a thank you for helping clean the room. Jan turned and headed back, thoughts of Sheriff Ray banished.

She made it back to The Elusive Cat with enough time left before dinner to catch a quick swim. Then she enjoyed a lovely dinner with Lois. Her sister had made a delicious fettuccine Alfredo with fresh local seafood. Accompanying it was a Caesar salad. Jan had seconds of everything. "That was wonderful, Lois," she exclaimed.

"Glad you enjoyed it. You know, I like cooking for someone again. Except for the occasional friend, I haven't cooked for another since Mom died."

Jan remembered her earlier thoughts. "Sorry I wasn't here to help you with her."

"You had your work and we were fine. You know we always got along. The doctor was good and the palliative nurse was great. They let her stay in her room until the end, although by then she was drugged up most of the time. Cancer is not a good way to die. Too bad that Maine doesn't allow doctor-assisted death. The last weeks are brutal on everyone."

"I heard they're discussing that in Canada now. And it's been legal in some parts of Europe for years. It makes sense. I mean, we allow our pets to die with dignity. We should let people have that right, too." Jan looked at her sister. "I guess we have to be careful. I mean, both parents have died from cancer. That really increases our risk."

"If you got cancer and it was terminal, would you choose suicide if you could?"

"I think I would. Never really thought about it but it is my life and I would like to control how I end it. And you?"

"Don't know. Don't want to go through what they went through but I really don't know. Suicide has always been so wrong. Look at Mr. Ellersby, or Marston, or whatever. He's bound to have family and friends who mourn him. And his death has sure caused us problems."

"If it was suicide," Jan said.

"Sheriff Ray told me yesterday that the police have decided that it was."

Jan didn't want to get into this discussion with her sister yet. She still had to sort out her facts. So she said, "Did you know that the Traegers decided not to have children because both her mother and brother died of cancer?"

"She's such a nice lady. I think they would have been great parents. But I guess we each make our own choices. I wonder if she's worried about herself," Lois said.

"She's already over sixty and looks to be in good health. Hopefully, she'll be fine. But I guess she's had to deal with the possibility. She told me that both of them had liver cancer."

"That's the worst. Maybe that makes her risk higher because they both had the same kind."

"I heard that everyone carries cancer cells within them but they are only activated in certain people. Not sure if it is organ specific or just luck of the draw which organ it grows in."

"I just try to be careful," Lois said. "You know about eating and such. And preventative care, of course. I hope that you are getting regular screenings from your doctor."

"I'm not dumb, Lois," Jan threw back. "I take care of myself, too."

"You should go to my doctor here, if you're staying awhile."

"Yeah, okay. I'll do that." She picked up their plates and carried them to the dishwasher. "Was anyone around today?"

"Ms. Lolinda was here until about 5:00. Guess she went to find dinner. The Traegers and Tiptons all said they would be going straight to dinner. They'll probably be back around 8:00. The Traegers leave just after lunch tomorrow. Their plane leaves around 5:00 p.m., I think. The new guest arrives Monday morning."

"Well, thank you for dinner. I'll go back to my place for a bit and probably drop in around 8:00."

"See you then."

Jan walked slowly back to the guest house. She was surprised to see Kitty Jr. waiting near the door. He watched her approach and then ran off before she got there. "Someday, you should drop in and stay for a bit," she called after him.

Once again, she turned to the computer. The three scenarios were still open: suicide; death by stranger; death by one of them staying at the B&B. She couldn't dismiss out of hand the sheriff's verdict. After all, he probably had access to information that she didn't. Maybe it was suicide. She built a 'pro' and 'con' column. She sat staring at the wall while she sorted through the reasons for suicide. She had personally only dealt with teenagers - attending information sessions on how to recognize the signs in children. It was hard to tell here because she hadn't known him before he came. Was he finding it daunting to live the rest of his life under a false name? In another country? Was embezzlement a serious enough crime for him to be hunted around the globe? Seemed unlikely, after all, half a million wasn't that much nowadays. If he got a fake passport and made it to Germany, he should have been free and clear. So why would he kill himself?

She tried to imagine living life under an assumed name far from friends and family. It actually sounded kind of liberating. You could create your own role. Be whoever you wanted to be. If he were divorced as Lolinda claimed, then he might not have any family. But what about parents? Siblings? She opened the family tree site and started putting in what she knew. Ted Marston born between 1952 and 1958. That should do for a start. She also put in Missouri to help narrow the search. There was nothing. She broadened the search to include nearby states. Still nothing. Then she removed the dates completely and just searched for the name. The professor showed up but she could eliminate him. She scrolled through screen after screen of document listings. She started at 1952 and just checked each one. Her eyes were starting to blur and then she found it. A legal name change. Ted Marston had been born Eddie Mason of Las Vegas, Nevada. He had already put one stage of his life behind him. It was unlikely that he would stress over doing it again. Suicide was not making any kind of sense. That left murder.

Chapter 8

Had Sheriff Ray found this document? Why was he so fixed on suicide? What if he had found the needle? Or knew that Ellersby had the drug? Was that conclusive?

First of all, the needle. If it had been found on the beach, that could indicate either murder or suicide. Not a deciding factor. And how could he know if Ellersby had the drug? Found a prescription? Jan went back to the internet and researched how to obtain barbiturates. Soon she was satisfied. It was not possible for a regular citizen to obtain these legally, not in the amount needed for a fatal overdose. They were only available from illicit drug dealers or to pharmacies. So there would be no prescription. Had they found evidence of a drug dealer? When? Where? In Acadia Park? Possible, but how had he made contact and why, when he was arranging documents to go to Germany?

No matter which way she twisted and turned it, she couldn't make suicide fit. So that made it murder. But Sheriff Ray said that the investigation was closed. Maybe she should just leave it. What right did she have to shake things up? He had been a criminal, escaping justice for his crime. He had come here to hide while planning to flee overseas. He had abandoned his old life and his family to run with the money. Was his death really a loss to anyone?

For some reason, this line of thinking angered her. She closed the computer and walked back to the beach. She wasn't surprised to find the kitten waiting for her. "You always know when I need someone to talk to." Jan went right down to the water's edge. It was halfway between low and high tide. She sat just out of reach of the waves, as though daring them to get her. The little gray cat stayed up higher with more dry sand between him and the water. "You live on the beach but you hate water."

She sat for a moment and then pounded her hand into the sand. "Why is life always so complicated?! Why can't I just sit on the beach and watch the waves?" As expected, the kitten didn't answer. "I know. I know. This is all my fault. I started it. I admit it. I saw this as a puzzle, something to distract me from Greg. It was just a game. But it's not a game. A man died and now I have learned things which could ruin another person's life. I should just let it be. A bad man is dead. Justice is satisfied."

The cat gave a small meow.

"Don't say that!" Jan told it. "I don't want to hear it. Sometimes murder is justified!"

The cat licked its paw and meowed again.

179

"You just won't let it go, will you? Okay, I will ask the question: did Mr. Ellersby deserve to die? That's really the point, isn't it? People kill in war. People kill in self-defense. But he wasn't hurting anyone, except maybe the company that he stole from. But if they have offices all over the US then I don't think his minor theft would be that harmful. He wasn't threatening anyone. All he wanted to do was leave quietly and start his life over somewhere else. That's exactly what I did. I mean I didn't commit a crime but I walked away. Maybe there isn't much of a parallel but I can understand him a bit. The desire to just dump the whole mess and leave. Should I deserve to die because I betrayed people's expectations? Aside from the stealing, isn't that what he did?"

"Who are you talking to?" a voice said behind her.

Jan spun around to see Brad walking towards her. "Kitty Jr. He's a very good listener."

Brad nodded. "Guess he doesn't interrupt too much."

"Come to watch the waves?" Jan asked.

"Just waiting until everyone else comes back down. Hoping to play *Monopoly* again. Will you play?"

"I'm hopeless at that game. Always have been," Jan replied. "Have a seat."

He sat near her. "You're going to get wet soon. The tide is coming in."

"I'm daring the waves to get me."

He looked at her strangely. "That's a silly dare. Of course they're going to get you."

Jan laughed. "But until they do, there's always a chance."

"No there isn't. Nothing is going to stop the tide coming in. If we sit here much longer, we will get wet. For certain."

"And that's probably why you like *Monopoly*."

"What do you mean? That makes no sense. What do the waves have to do with the game?"

"As you may have realized, there are several different ways to look at life."

"This is beginning to sound like school," the boy smiled.

"That will teach you to never ask a teacher a question. We can't help it. Shall I continue?"

"Okay."

"I promise it won't be on the exam," Jan teased. They both laughed. "Some people see life as a road, a pathway, with obstacles and adventures. So they plot their course, assessing risk and moving ahead. But others see it as a random open field, filled with all sorts of delights and fears. They just keep romping through the grass hoping that the next discovery is a good one."

"But that's silly," Brad said. "You'll never get anywhere if you don't plan."

"Which is why you're great at *Monopoly* and I'm a hopeless disaster. You're planning your empire and I'm dancing through the flowers, forgetting that I have to pay rent wherever I land."

"Really? That sounds...I don't know...not right. For an adult, I mean."

"Do you know why it doesn't sound right? Because it doesn't take into account being responsible for our own actions. In the game, if I flit all over the place, I go bankrupt. Life has consequences, too."

A wave came up and they had to scramble to get out of its way. "The tide's coming in," Brad declared. "What you said sounds messed up. I thought teachers were supposed to explain things."

Jan laughed again. "Kitty Jr. wasn't too impressed either. But then, I'm not a teacher. I'm a pot scrubber sitting on a beach talking to a kitten and daring the waves to catch me." Her grin grew bigger at the expression on the boy's face. "Don't try to figure it out, Brad. Go beat someone at your game and have fun. You've got a good brain and you're on the right path."

"You sure you're okay, Jan?"

"I'm fine. Just some evening musings with a cat. Go on. I'll be by later to see how it's going."

"Don't get wet," he said as he got to his feet.

She laughed. Then she had to leap to her feet as a particularly big wave came in. "Got the message," she said to the water. "I'll go in now." As she walked to the house, she looked for the kitten but it was nowhere in sight.

The Traegers were sitting at a table looking out at the beach. The sun had long set and the ocean was dark. They didn't seem to be talking much as Jan went into the kitchen, where Lois was doing some baking. "What are you working on now?"

"Just preparing the dough for fresh cinnamon buns in the morning. If I start it now, I don't have to get up at 4:30 a.m."

"Can I help?"

"I can't ask you to clean up after me twenty-four-seven," Lois said.

"But I can offer. I think Brad's starting another *Monopoly* game and I need an excuse to delay going in there."

"You never liked that game. Your favorite was *Clue*, wasn't it?"

Jan grabbed a dishcloth and started wiping down the counter. "I'd forgotten that. You didn't like that one."

"'Cause you always beat me."

"Which is why I didn't like *Monopoly*. You always won. Strange how life is reflected in the board games we chose as children."

"What do you mean?"

"Just something I was discussing with Brad. About the different ways that people approach life."

"Are you okay, Jan?"

"Still figuring that out, Big Sister. I'll see if the Traegers want any tea." She went near the older couple and made her offer.

Herr Traeger shook his head but Frau Traeger was pleased. "That would be lovely, Jan."

When Jan returned with the cup and saucer, she asked, "How was your day?"

"It was good," Herr Traeger said. "It is surprising how proud Americans are of their history when they are such a young country. We walked through a historic house preserved from 1898. My parents' home was built in 1882 and is just considered an old home. We have a church in Trier, Germany which was completed in the twelfth century. Now that's history."

Jan laughed. "Well, I guess we have to make do with what we have. In the twelfth century, there was no United States, just native tribes. The only thing that we have from that far back might be some arrowheads."

"Now, mein lieber, don't be so critical," Frau Traeger said. "I loved the house and it's nice to see a country proud of its accomplishments."

"Didn't mean anything by that, Ms. Jan," he apologized.

"No offense taken. Just puts things in perspective, I guess. I'd love to see a twelfth century church. I can't imagine anything surviving that long. My apartment in San Francisco was built in the 1960s and was already falling apart."

Herr Traeger said, "You should come to Germany. It is a beautiful country."

"I'd like to do that someday."

Jan went back to the kitchen but found that Lois had finished and left. So she went into the family room. She was relieved to see that the game was already under way. Brad had accumulated some properties, while his sister and mother were struggling. He grinned up at her as she looked at the game. She just smiled and went to make sure the coffee and juice were fully stocked. She saw Scott Tipton looking over a brochure for deep sea fishing.

He looked up at her. "Judy said you recommended this. Thanks. It looks great."

"I heard you're quite the sailor."

"I love the ocean. My parents always brought us here when we were kids. I wanted our kids to have the same experience. But it's a lot of work and responsibility to take care of a boat. For every hour on the water it seems like there are two hours of dockside work. I just don't have the time. Not now with the kids. I think we should just get a taxi sign and stick it on top of the car. Between sports events, friends, and social things, we seem to be spending most of the year carting the kids around. Of course, Judy bears most of the burden but I help out on the weekends. No time for the boat. It was time to sell it." He smiled at her. "But it's in my blood. I'll get another when the kids learn to drive themselves. But in the meantime, this should be amazing."

He checked the room and lowered his voice. "I understand from Judy that Lois had a tragedy connected to a deep sea fishing expedition. Lost her husband?"

"Four years ago. It was a freak autumn storm. Came from nowhere. The boat went down with all hands."

"I'll tell the kids to be discreet about this trip."

"Thanks," Jan said. "If everything's fine here, I think I'll turn in."

"We're fine." There was a groan from Josie at the table. He laughed. "Really, we are. Good night, Jan."

She smiled and went over to the table. "Good night, all. And Brad, be merciful."

"What's that?" he grinned.

She lightly slapped his head and left, laughing.

When she got to the guest house, she was surprised to see Lolinda's door open. She popped her head in. "I didn't know you were back."

The actress smiled. "I came back while you were talking to Kitty Jr. How'd the discussion go?"

"Kitty is a hard taskmaster. She doesn't let me get away with anything."

"Come in and have a seat. What are you trying to get away with?"

Jan sat on the end of the bed. Lolinda was in the comfortable chair near the window, a book on her lap. "Running from responsibility. What else?"

"That doesn't work, does it? It follows us around no matter what we do."

"Yeah, Kitty said the same thing."

"I won't pry. I know you'll make the right decision. What I'm really curious about is whether or not you found an art class?"

"I met Steve at the Art of Being and he is willing to take the dare. He has no clue what he's getting himself into. But I will be there on Wednesday afternoon for my first session with a class of beginner adults. Not my fault if he finds me hopeless."

"Have you ever had a hopeless student?"

Jan smiled. "No. Some just take more work."

"Well, there you go. More work and more time. What will you paint?"

"He's starting me with apples. Shapes first and then fruit."

"Good idea. Best way to start. So what do you want to paint? Landscapes? There are some beautiful views around here."

"Actually - cats."

Lolinda burst out laughing. "I might have known. You and Kitty Jr. Quite the pair."

Jan stood up, smiling. "I'll let you get back to your book. Good night, Ms. Lolinda."

"Good night, Jan."

Jan went back to her room and opened the computer but didn't have anything else to look up. She had all the information. She just needed to decide what to do with it. She turned off the light and tried to sleep but it was no good. Her brain wouldn't leave her alone. Grabbing the sweat pants again, she thought that this was getting to be a habit. She knew that the kitten would be waiting to continue their interrupted discussion.

This time she walked a bit down the beach, away from the point around which lay the other cottages. The B&B was on a bit of an inlet. There was another cottage beside them, going north, but there hadn't been anyone there since she had arrived in July. She shined her small flashlight on the sand, staying above the rising tide. When the lights from the B&B were only a glow in the distance, she found a smooth space of sand and sat down. As she glanced back at the lights, she saw a small gray shadow trotting along. As the kitten approached, she said quietly, "Can't escape you, can I? Just like I can't escape myself. Ran halfway across the country and still ended up with...what? A mind that couldn't just let life be."

But life wasn't something that happened to one. Life was what we made it. And she had made her life a mess. She had run from California and its disaster only to create another one here. Why her? She took a deep breath. She remembered something that a friend had told her years ago. Not a close friend, just another teacher, who taught the senior class. She had said that if something keeps happening to you then you should look at yourself. They had been talking about bullying patterns. How children can escape a bullying situation and then find themselves in another one. Same thing happened to women escaping abusive relationships only to fall into another. This teacher had said that some people identified themselves as victims, so they only felt validated when they were in the victim role.

Jan had wondered about that and studied more carefully the relationships among her students. She knew that, as preteens, they were searching for their own identities. However she had never thought that someone would choose the identity of a victim. And, of course, it wasn't that simple, but she did start to see some patterns. And the other thing she noticed is that identities grew out of past experiences. If someone only knew bullying, then

191

bullies were their familiars. Like those poor kids who grow up in war-torn countries and don't know any other way.

So what did that make her? She wasn't a victim, in either situation - Greg or here. And she hadn't been a victim at home. Sure, her mom hadn't understood her but that happened all the time. She had known that she was loved. She had been well cared for. So what was her problem?

When she looked at her actions - the prom, missing graduation, moving to California, breaking it off with Greg - she did start to see a pattern. In each case, someone was trying to force her to fit a mold, play a role. And she had a mule's reaction to that. Fight against it even if it was in her best interest. This had definitely been true for both the prom and graduation. She now regretted not doing these properly. But California and Greg were different. There, the rebellions had led to good things. California had given her a new perspective and new hope. Greg had shown her what she didn't want, and had clarified her identity.

Did any of this have anything to do with the present situation? Her only role here was as the sister of the owner of The Elusive Cat. No one expected any more of her. But she expected more of herself. And Lois did, too, even if that was based on their mother's expectations.

Why did it bother her so much when Lois said she was smarter? She was. She couldn't deny it. If smart was based on IQ, then she was smarter. Didn't make her wiser. And destined for more than wife and mother? She was that, too. At least for something different if not 'more.' It bothered her because it meant that she couldn't just dance her way through life, running when it got too messy. She had to take responsibility, not only for her actions but for who she was. And she didn't want to.

"There, it's out in the open," she told her silent listener. "I want someone to take responsibility for shaping and forming me, and yet I resist whenever anyone tries to do just that. What a mess! But enough self-pity. What should I do about Mr. Ellersby? That's what we need to decide tonight, because it's the last night. People start to scatter tomorrow."

She looked back down the beach toward the house. "I think I came this far down the beach this evening so I could get away from him - from where he died. But it doesn't do any good. To answer my earlier question: did he deserve to die? No, he didn't deserve to die. And he does deserve justice. Everyone needs to take responsibility for their actions. I will call Sheriff Ray first thing in the morning."

She looked over to see the cat curled up into a ball, sleeping. "Guess I'll do the same, but in my warm bed this time. Good night, Kitty Jr. Thanks for listening."

Although her decision had been made, she didn't find it easy to fall asleep. She couldn't help thinking about the possible consequences of her decision. It was easy to say that people should pay for their actions. It was harder when you knew, and liked, the person who will have to pay. She finally drifted off and dreamt of waves, cats, apples, and hangman's nooses. It was not a restful night.

She awoke around 6:30 a.m. It was still too early to call the sheriff but Lois should be up. The sun had just appeared over the horizon and was painting the tips of the waves. She looked along the beach but couldn't see the kitten. She even checked behind the house but neither the little one nor his more elusive mother were anywhere in sight. She was on her own. She quietly let herself into the main house.

Lois was working in the kitchen, rolling and cutting the last of the cinnamon buns. The oven was already on and the kitchen felt warm and familiar. "You're up early," her sister remarked.

"Decided to check out the sunrise."

"It is dramatic over the ocean," Lois agreed. "I can watch it through the windows here."

"You don't go in the ocean much, do you?" Jan realized.

"No, swimming was never my thing. But you should see Johnny. He would be in the water all day, if he could. A fish. Always was like that. So was John. I love to look at it but that's it." She popped the pans into the hot oven. "Any plans for today?"

"Just waiting to see what comes up. You?"

"Probably get started on the Traegers' room once they leave. Have to remind Frau Traeger about her medicine in the fridge."

"Did she remember to take it this week?" Jan asked.

"Yes, she came in here one morning early and took a dose from the bag. The new gentleman is from Oregon. He seems friendly enough. First time to the East Coast."

"Don't you ever get tired of the constant stream of strangers in your house?"

Lois shook her head, as she started to boil water for poached eggs. "I like the variety. They're all different.

It's like I get to share a bit of their lives but never have to get really involved. I do like it."

"Even if they all ask the same questions: where can we rent a boat? What's a good place to eat?"

Lois laughed. "They do that, for sure. But that's fine. I try to have a selection of brochures. Whenever a new venue opens up, I try to get some of their brochures. Of course, several businesses in the town actively recruit the B&B owners. I'm happy to put out their pamphlets but I don't recommend unless I've been there myself. You're helping with that because you get around more than I do. I heard you recommending specific trails to the men a few days ago. I haven't had time to do much hiking. And the only place I seem to spend much time in town is the grocery store."

"We really need to work on getting you out more, dear sister. It's a nice little town. Wonder if the art store has anything for the tourists?"

"Why don't you ask at your next class?" Lois teased.

"Maybe I will." Jan heard footsteps coming down the stairs. It was Brad and Josie. "Decided not to wait for the parents for breakfast?" she asked smiling.

They nodded. "But only if it's ready, Ms. Lois," Josie said.

"Give me twenty minutes and it will be done."

"Sure. Then we'll go along the beach."

"Tell me if you see either of the cats. They weren't out this morning."

"'Kay." The kids left.

"Why'd you ask about the cats?" Lois said.

"Just curious. Kitty Jr. usually greets me but he wasn't there this morning."

"Probably chasing his breakfast. I didn't know that he greeted you. Getting friendlier than his mom. In the four years that I've been here, she has never let me near her."

"Oh, he won't let me pet him but he likes to watch the waves with me."

"Cats hate water."

Jan nodded. "Guess he's like you. Loves the waves but not the water. Guess I'd better start setting the tables. I need to make a private phone call first. Okay if I use your room?"

"Sure."

Jan closed the door firmly and walked over to the window, while pulling out her cell phone. She still hesitated a moment before dialing the number of the police station. She hoped that Ray was in by now. She was put on hold for a bit but then heard his voice. "How can I help you, Ms. Cathcart?"

She flinched at the formality but she couldn't do anything about that. She had worked out what she would say. "Sheriff Ray, you asked me for solid evidence. Well, I have it or, at least, I know where it can be found but I need you to get it. I can tell you for a fact that Mr. Ellersby did not commit suicide. He was murdered and I know the identity of the murderer."

There was silence on the line. "Ms. Cathcart, do you know what you're saying?"

"Yes, Sheriff Nolan, I do. I know what I've seen and heard this week and I know what has happened. I would appreciate some help so that justice is done. All I ask is that you come to The Elusive Cat this morning with two of your constables."

"Two of them? So this person is violent?"

"I don't think so. No, I need someone to take the two children out of here before you make your arrest. They shouldn't be here for that."

Another long pause and then Jan knew that he was at least willing to hear her out. "Constable Phelps has his sailboat just around the bay from you. He could take the kids out on that. Are you sure this is necessary?"

"I won't reveal anything in front of those children. They've been through enough this week. And it is necessary that you be here with backup."

"Just tell me what you know and I will handle this. It is a police matter."

"I know that, sir, which is why I came by your office yesterday. Then I had suspicions, now I know for sure. So please be here in about an hour. We will have finished breakfast by then. Just knock and come in and join the guests when you arrive."

"Now, see here, Jan. You're getting awfully sure of yourself," his voice rose.

"I'm doing what needs to be done, Ray. I have to go help Lois. Please be here." She hung up the phone to find her hands trembling. She couldn't figure out if it was fear that she was wrong or fear that she was right. She put her phone in her pocket and took a couple of deep breaths. She didn't want Lois to get suspicious. This was her task and she would complete it alone.

Chapter 9

Jan went back into the kitchen and grabbed the silverware for the tables. She started to set them up as her mind ran over the conversation. What if he didn't come? What would she do then? But he had to come. He wasn't that arrogant, was he? A bit patronizing but a good police officer. She had to trust that he would be here. And he had a good solution for her problem of what to do with the kids. She didn't want them to learn about all the gruesomeness of life just yet. Finding a corpse on the beach was enough for one vacation. She reminded herself to check in with Brad next week. They weren't leaving until the end of that week so she had time. But he seemed to be doing well.

If this all happened, one thing was sure. Ray would never again think of her as the dishwashing little sister of The Elusive Cat. And Lois would be shocked, too. Which wasn't all bad. Lois still held the image of her as a child. The last time they had lived together, she had been fourteen. Then Lois had married John and moved out of the house. A lot had happened since then. And Lois would just have to deal with who she had become.

Then she thought about Steve's rumor mill and Richard at the park. How would they view her? They had all been happy, or at least had accepted, the verdict of suicide. She would make it murder. She would shake up the little town. Would she have to leave? Again?

"I agree it is a nice beach," Lois interrupted her. "But the guests will be down soon. Could you stop staring out the window and finish with the tables?"

"Sorry," Jan mumbled. She quickly put the rest of the forks and knives in place and got some napkins from the holder to fold and put around. But her mind kept going. She didn't want to leave. Not yet. And she was through with running. At least, she thought she was. It depended on how ugly it got.

She looked up to hear more footsteps. This time it was the Traegers. They sat at their usual table. "Breakfast in five minutes," Jan said. "But the coffee is ready."

"That would be fine," Herr Traeger replied. "Thank you, Jan."

She fetched them coffee and went back into the kitchen. She took the platters as Lois filled them and put them on the pass-through counter. The Tiptons came down soon and Scott went to the door to call for the children. Soon breakfast was proceeding as usual, except the Traegers' table was free from brochures. They would be spending the morning packing to leave just after lunch.

When all the food was out and everyone was served, Jan still stood watching. She had her cup of coffee but didn't think she could eat anything. Her stomach was knotted. The sheriff would be here soon. She was about to destroy people's lives. That's what she had decided to do. It didn't help to keep saying that the murderer started all this. That they had brought it to this conclusion. She couldn't escape responsibility for what she was about to do. If she had never called Ray, if she had stayed silent, they would have just gone on with their lives and Mr. Ellersby would have been quietly buried.

"You're miles away, today, Jan. What's up?" Lois was looking at her.

"Did you read Edgar Allen Poe in high school? That one about the beating heart?"

"Where'd that come from?"

"Do you remember it?"

"Yeah. The teacher played this creepy rock-style musical version of it. That's why I remember it. Why?"

"Do you think it's true? Do you think people's conscience torments them if they do something terrible?"

"This is a very strange conversation, Jan. Even for you. But to answer your question, I guess it depends on whether or not they have a conscience."

"Most people do. I don't mean psychopaths but regular people. We're plagued by things we've done in the past. People we've hurt. Don't you agree?"

"I guess so. I never thought much about it. Does this have something to do with Mr. Ellersby?"

"Sort of."

"Do you think he killed himself because he felt guilty for taking that money?"

"I don't know how he felt about that. I didn't know him well enough." She regretted starting the conversation. She just wanted someone to reassure her that she was doing the right thing. "Oh, I just remembered that I promised Ms. Lolinda that I would get her early. Be right back." With that she ran out of the house.

At the guest house, she was pleased and surprised to see the light on under the actress' door. She knocked and it was opened shortly. Lolinda was already dressed. "Good morning, Jan. What brings you here?"

"I'm so glad you're up and dressed. Sheriff Ray will be coming by soon and wanted everyone in the breakfast room."

"Okay, I'll walk over there with you now. Wonder what this is all about. Do you know?"

But Jan just headed quickly out the door, leading the way to the main house and not letting the woman ask any more questions.

Lolinda went in and greeted everyone. Then she went and got a cinnamon roll and some coffee. The Tiptons were showing signs of getting ready to leave. Jan said, "Sorry to bother you but the sheriff called this morning and wondered if you would all please just wait a few minutes for him."

Lois said to her quietly, "When did he call? I know nothing about this."

"Sorry, it was while I was in your room. I meant to tell you." She was getting nervous. What if he didn't show after all? Then she gave a slight sigh as she saw three men in uniform come around the side of the house. They came in and looked at her. She motioned Ray to an empty seat at the round table with the Traegers. She brought him some coffee. The constables stayed at the door. She went back into the kitchen while everyone waited for the sheriff to speak. He, alone, looked at her.

She came to the counter, keeping it between herself and the group. She could feel Lois looking at her from behind. "I'm sorry for a bit of a deception. I'm really the one who asked you all to be here, although Sheriff Ray has agreed. I would like to ask a favor of Brad and Josie." She turned to the two of them. "I know that you are curious and you will hear the story from me later, but for now I need to speak with the adults. Constable Phelps has offered to take you two out on his sailing boat for a bit. It will be a lot more exciting than sitting here."

Judy Tipton looked at Jan and then nodded. "Off you go, guys. Listen to the constable and have fun." With a last look at their mother, the kids left with the constable.

Everyone looked back at Jan. "For these last five days, we have all been shadowed by the ghost of Mr. Ellersby's death. The sheriff and his men have been working hard with the help of authorities across the country to solve this crime. Living here with all of you but being a bit separate, since I am neither your host nor a guest, I have learned things which I think can help the sheriff so that we can move on."

"Based on various people's observations and my own, I determined that Mr. Ellersby had to have died between 9:00 and 11:00 p.m. on Tuesday. These times are set by our schedules and the tides. When I left to go to my room it was 9:00 p.m. The petit fours that Lois had saved for Mr. Ellersby were still sitting on the counter. That gives us our earliest time because the coroner found evidence that he had indeed eaten the petit fours. Now the high tide comes in just after 11:00 p.m. His body was found below the high-water mark. I think it is safe to assume that he did not sit down in the water, fully dressed as he was. Therefore he sat down there before 11:00 p.m."

Sheriff Ray nodded. "This agrees with the coroner's report."

"Thank you." Jan continued, "Now Ms. Lolinda returned that night, from time spent with friends, around midnight and she would have usually seen him lying on the beach but she didn't. It so happened that her flashlight battery had burnt out and she had to make her way to the guest house in the dark. So her attention was solely on her feet staying on the pathway. If you remember, there was very little moon five nights ago. So she didn't see him. And by then he was dead. The police have determined that it was poison. Although they haven't given us any details, I believe that it was some form of barbiturate, the kind used in euthanasia. It would have given him a peaceful death."

She looked at the sheriff, who once again nodded. "I thought it might be suicide. I really hoped it might be suicide but I no longer think that it was. There were a couple of things bothering me. First, where would he have gotten the drugs? And secondly, if he were going to kill himself, why would he meet with someone to arrange for a fake passport just that evening."

Everyone, including the sheriff looked at her in surprise. "I found this out by accident almost. I heard that Mr. Ellersby had visited the art shop in town the evening before he died. That struck me as strange. Not just because I didn't know that he was interested in art. Anyone can be. But because he was fleeing from the police and trying to hide. He would not have taken the time to buy art supplies. And, in fact, he didn't buy any. I checked with the owner. I also found out from him that Mr. Ellersby had met a man at the store. I don't have confirmation, although I'm sure the sheriff will be able to find it, that this man will supply documents for a fee. Does that sound like a man preparing to die?"

She looked around the room but no one moved. They were all staring at her. She had a moment of panic but knew that she had to continue. She just hoped that she was right. "So, I ruled out suicide, which left murder. As you already know, Mr. Ellersby's name was actually Ted Marston. There is a warrant out for his arrest for embezzlement. Mr. Tipton works for the same company at its headquarters in San Francisco, however Mr. Tipton only found this out from the sheriff. He hadn't known it before because his vacation started before the memo was sent around about Marston's crime. And his family won't let him do work on vacation." She smiled at the couple who smiled tentatively back.

"By the time Ted Marston and his partner were suspected, nearly two weeks ago, they had managed to steal over a million dollars from the company. They split the money and ran. His partner was picked up but Marston got out of the state. He ended up here with a suitcase full of money - half a million dollars - which he stored in the secret cubbyhole which is in each of the closets. He had overheard Brad and Lois discussing them and had made good use of his. Sheriff Ray found the case there with some money. But not half a million dollars. In fact, there was slightly less than half of that in the bag. And that was the real mystery. Why was there only half? If someone had stolen it, why not all? If Marston himself had stashed it somewhere, again, why not all or most? What was significant about half?"

Jan took a sip of her cooling coffee. Now for the hard part. "I need to digress here for a moment to discuss motive. Greed was an obvious one. There are few of us who wouldn't be helped by a sudden influx of half a million dollars. But greed would have taken all, not half. If no one knew who he was and what he'd done, they wouldn't have known the cash was there for taking. And if someone from outside knew that he was here, they would have taken all the money, if they could have found it. No, greed wasn't the motive."

She looked around to see if they were still following her. They waited for her next words. "The motive was, I believe, justice. Someone here, by the strangest of coincidences, knew who Marston was. Recognized him from a photograph. And knew that he was a bad man. Knew that he cheated and lied and betrayed those who loved him. But he had escaped any punishment and was about to escape further. He had discussed moving to Germany. He was going to move out of reach from justice of any kind."

"And so they took matters into their own hands. For justice had to be served. They had the means - hypodermic needles for injecting the poison into the petit fours on the counter. They had the drug - carrying it as a safeguard against a horrible death. They had the motive. Ted Marston had betrayed the dearest person in their life. Had left that person destitute, with the care of young children, and had run away with his fortune."

She paused and looked at the sheriff. He straightened himself up and looked around. "Half is the amount usually settled on a spouse during a divorce proceeding. Half is what was taken to be given to the victim of his stealing. Not his company but his former spouse."

Jan took a deep breath. "Frau Traeger, your niece lives in Missouri, doesn't she? Your niece, Jennifer Marston, former wife of Ted Marston. Your niece whose maiden name is Turcotte, the same as yours. She is the daughter of your late brother, is she not? The girl you said was more like a daughter to you."

Everyone stared at the older woman but she was only looking at Jan. She forced herself to continue, meeting those eyes. "Although you weren't invited to the wedding, you did have the picture. You recognized Mr. Ellersby as the man who had abandoned your niece. And you had also heard about the secret hidden spaces. I think your intention had been just to kill him so that he wouldn't hurt her or anyone else ever again. But then you searched his room, probably to make sure there were no references to your niece. I imagine you were relieved and angered when you found none. Then you checked the closet. I can imagine your surprise when you found a suitcase full of money. Then you thought of a real way to help your niece. You would take her half and give it to her."

There was total silence in the room. Jan noticed that the constable was no longer at the door. He was quietly making his way up the stairs. Sheriff Ray had stood up but it was her husband who broke the silence. "Hilde? What is she saying? What's she mean?"

"He was Jennifer's husband," his wife said quietly to him. "Staying here. Under a false name. As if he could escape responsibility. And then he asked you about life in Germany. Can't you understand? He was going to get away with it! His poor children. And Jennifer."

"Jen's husband? Why didn't you tell me?" he stumbled.

Hilde Traeger smiled at him, laying a hand on his. "I couldn't, Rolf. You were so excited about searching for your American family. I couldn't drag you into the mess that my family is. You were to stay untouched by all this. But he was an evil man and I have no regrets."

Sheriff Ray took over. "I would like to ask everyone but the Traegers to please go into the back room. Lois, I'm sure you and Jan can arrange for coffee. We will keep you as short a time as possible." Scott Tipton was the first to move and the others slowly followed, looking at the seated gray-haired lady as they went.

Lois got the coffee and fixings. Jan followed with the cups and spoons, but her hands were shaking. The door was closed behind her. Everyone just stood looking at each other. Lois put down the coffee and started the machine. Judy came over to Jan. "What just happened?"

"I'm sorry. I'm so sorry." Judy took the cups before they fell.

Lois put her arm around her sister and led her to the couch, sitting beside her. "Just deep breaths, Jan. You'll be okay." She stared at her for a moment. "Is that why you asked about Poe?"

Jan's voice was quiet. "She's such a nice lady. I was hoping that maybe her conscience was bothering her and she would be better if she were found out. I didn't want to hurt her."

"How did you know, Jan?" Judy asked.

"I heard the rumor in town about suicide and it was all wrong. The pieces didn't fit. And I couldn't move past the money. Half just didn't make any kind of sense."

"When did you know?" Lois asked.

"Not for sure until yesterday. I mean I had all the pieces but they came together yesterday evening."

"Your conversation with Kitty Jr.," Lolinda said quietly.

Jan nodded. The others just looked at each other. "I think you should start at the beginning," Scott Tipton said.

"I noticed when we found the body that there was no water in his mouth. Brad noticed it, too. I felt pretty sure that he hadn't drowned, so I was looking for other ways right from the start. Then Ray told Lois and me that he had been poisoned and the last thing in his stomach was the petit fours. Well, I knew that Lois hadn't poisoned him." She smiled slightly at her sister who pressed her hand. "So I began to do some research on poisons. As Sheriff Ray just confirmed, it was a barbiturate and those are usually administered by needle. I reasoned that Ellersby wouldn't have sat quietly while someone injected him so I thought maybe the poison had been injected into the petit fours. Either way, it requires a needle."

"And Frau Traeger has needles for her weekly injections," Lois said.

"Right. Maybe they'll find two used needles in her room, instead of the one she used on herself. And in a conversation about her family, she mentioned that both her mother and brother died of liver cancer. She remarked on how horrible that was. It was the reason they didn't have children. And she told me that she wouldn't want to die like that. So I thought that maybe she had managed to get some drug which would induce a death, like for doctor-assisted deaths. I couldn't verify that, but she seemed the only one that might have a drug like that. I looked it up and Germany doesn't really allow it but they are familiar with it. And Holland has allowed it for years. She could have had access. She could have gotten it to use on herself if needed."

"You've done a lot of research," Scott commented.

"I had to get all the facts to put it together. I had the means - anyone could have tampered with the petit fours since they were sitting on the counter, clearly marked. But only Frau Traeger had the needles and a likelihood of having a lethal dose on her. But I had no motive."

"One minute. How did you rule out suicide?" Scott asked.

"Initially, it just didn't sit right. He had gone to all this trouble to steal the money and travel across the country to hide here under a false name. And then I did more research. It turns out that this isn't the first time he changed his name. Although that time he did it legally. It was when he was eighteen and left home. So he was used to just leaving and moving on. I knew that he was divorced and I found the name of his wife. That's when it clicked."

"Yes, I didn't get that part of his ex being Frau Traeger's niece. How'd you figure that out?" Lois said.

"I had been discussing family histories with Herr Traeger. He was explaining that he wanted to find some records in New York. And then it came up with his wife. Can't remember how. I think we were discussing her husband. She said that her maiden name, Turcotte, originally came from France. After all my years as a school teacher, I hear a name once and it sticks. So when I was searching for Ted Marston on the internet it came up with a funeral announcement for his wife's mother. Last name, Turcotte."

"Wow," Lolinda said. "That's convoluted. No wonder you spent so much time on the computer."

"Well, there was also the fact that Frau Traeger had mentioned her daughter lived in Missouri. Marston also came from Missouri."

"As did we," Lois commented quietly.

Jan nodded. "That's why it stuck in my head. Everyone seems to have some connection to Missouri. So then we had that conversation at the restaurant about trust and betrayal."

"She spoke quite strongly about it."

"She had a brutal past," Lolinda said. "Her father abandoned them when they were little. Her mother and brother both died horrible early deaths from cancer. She only had one bright spot in her family and that was her niece. I believe that the adoration was one-sided. It was telling, Jan, that she wasn't invited to the niece's wedding."

Jan nodded. "If she had been then Herr Traeger would have recognized him, too."

Lois sighed. "Maybe he could have stopped her."

"I don't know. She felt deeply about the betrayal of trust," Jan said. "She felt that Marston had betrayed his family just as her father had. But it was the half the money that led me to the answer. Half makes no sense unless you consider the split between spouses. Do you remember that she also told us about their separate bank accounts? Each one had half their savings."

Judy nodded.

Jan looked around at all these now familiar faces watching her. "I'm so sorry that I had to do that to everyone but I had to convince Sheriff Ray. He wouldn't listen when I tried to give him some of the information. He just told me to leave it all to him."

"Something that irritated you," Lois commented quietly.

"I'll admit it did," Jan confirmed. "I've always looked after myself. I don't like being told to leave things to others when I can do something. I knew the stress that this was putting on you, Lois. And I knew that the police could never learn the things that I could. And, as I said, they wouldn't listen. So I had to present everything like this so that the sheriff would know and Frau Traeger would understand that he knew."

"I can't believe it. Such a sweet old lady," Judy said.

"I wonder what will happen to her," Lois asked.

"She'll go to jail," Scott said.

"Poor Herr Traeger," Lolinda said.

"And the money?" Judy asked.

"It will go back to the company," her husband answered. "After all, it is theirs."

"I wonder if the niece will ever know what her aunt did for her," Lois asked.

After a moment of silence, Lolinda said, "I'm not sure I would want to know that someone had killed for me."

Scott turned to get a cup of coffee and it broke up the circle. Lois, after a final hug for Jan, went to make sure everything on the table was fine. Lolinda took her place and took Jan's hand in both of hers. "I think I understand the nature of your conversation last night with Kitty. You did the right thing, Jan. As I knew you would."

Jan looked up, pleading, "Did I? A very nice lady is going to jail. Her equally wonderful husband has had his life torn apart. And Mr. Ellersby is dead and doesn't care about justice done in his name - whichever name he chooses."

"There must always be those who stand up for the silent. He deserved justice. And do you really think that Hilde Traeger could know a moment's peace with her terrible secret?"

"I don't know. She's acted so normal for the last several days. Maybe it didn't bother her."

"You don't believe that. I heard your sister's comment to you about Poe. By any chance, were you referring to 'The Tell-Tale Heart'?"

"How'd you know?"

"It is the most relevant. Good people have a conscience. A blessing and a curse. Even if Hilde could act normally with us, can you imagine the strain on her marriage? It would have ended in misery no matter what. This way it is out in the open. No matter what the consequences are, the deception is over. They can now deal with the reality."

"I hope you're right, Ms. Lolinda. You have such a clear way of seeing things. I'm always murky."

The actress turned and faced her squarely, pulling her around on the couch. "Ms. Jan, you are one of the most clearheaded people that I have ever known. That you noticed the lack of water in his mouth, when everyone else was probably standing around with their mouths hanging open in shock, is proof of that. And you are also one of the most courageous. Acting alone, you pursued justice, even in the face of opposition by the law. You did the right thing."

She paused and then moved one hand to Jan's shoulder. "Whatever you were running from, I'm glad you ran here. But I think you can now stop running. You may not stay here - Henry's Harbor's loss - but wherever you go it will be as a destination, not a sanctuary."

"I hope you're right."

"You know I am. And I'm sure Kitty Jr. would agree," Lolinda smiled.

Jan hugged her and said simply, "Thanks."

Conversation after that was quiet and random. Ray came after half an hour and said that they could go on with their days. He would be around later for some simple questions but the case was over. He told the Tiptons where they could find their children. Lolinda went back to her room, with a smile for Jan. Then the sheriff settled in the breakfast room with Jan and Lois. The Traegers were gone.

The sheriff looked at his coffee for a moment and then said, "I want to apologize to you, Jan. I should have listened when you came to my office. All I can say in defense is that I didn't know you."

"I understand," Jan said. "I was just the dishwashing younger sister."

"You are a lot more than that. You not only figured this out without any forensic help, but you saved the police department from making a serious mistake. I thank you."

"What will happen to Frau Traeger?" Lois asked.

"It's in the hands of the courts now. She made a full confession and we have the hypodermic needles, the empty bottle of barbiturates and the money from their room. Hopefully, given the circumstances, the judge will be lenient."

"And Herr Traeger?"

"He will stay here with her. I'm sure the immigration office will give him an extended visa on compassionate grounds."

"So he really knew nothing about what she'd done?"

"No, he was bowled over. He didn't have a clue," Ray confirmed. "Poor man." He stood up. "Well, I will leave you ladies. Thanks again, Jan. Maybe in the future we'll have a chance to get to know each other better. My fault that we got off on the wrong foot."

"Don't worry about it, Ray. You were doing your job. And maybe I'll stick around for a bit so we'll have a chance to grab a coffee."

"Jan's taking an art class in town," Lois said.

Ray looked impressed but Jan said, "We'll see how that goes. My drawing may be the worst crime of the century." They all smiled and the sheriff left.

Jan started to clear the tables. Lois just looked at her. "What?" Jan asked.

"I'd like a chance to get to know you better, too."

Jan grinned. "You may regret saying that, Big Sister. But I would love to stay here for a bit. And now, please let me get to work. I'm way behind schedule today."

Lois laughed and went to the kitchen. "By the way," she called. "You still haven't had breakfast. How many eggs do you want?"

Jan smiled. Maybe Lolinda was right and it would be okay. "Two would be fine. Thanks."

When breakfast was done and the kitchen was clean for the day, Jan walked out onto the beach. As she sat down in the sun, her faithful companion came trotting up. "There you are. I was afraid my talking scared you away last night. Glad to see you. And thanks for your help. Maybe one day you'll let me draw a picture of you."

The gray kitten meowed and Jan laughed.

Thanks for reading!
© Sara Bourgeois 2021

This story is a work of fiction. Any resemblance to persons alive or dead is a coincidence.

Made in the USA
Las Vegas, NV
02 November 2021